Climb The Tree

A novel by

Michael Bertrand

ISBN 978-0-578-59932-8

Cover by Paul A. Smith

The Manor

Orientation

They arrived thirty minutes early for their 10:00 appointment. "Early is on time and on time is late," was one of Richard's favorite sayings.

Charles didn't mind. He liked seeing his father happy. They spent their free time on a short walk outside.

"It's laid out in three rings," Richard explained. "The outer and middle rings are independent housing." He pointed to their left. "Two and three bedroom houses, just like the ones your gramps and granny live in. Most of them are occupied, and they're all in good shape." Richard pointed at the tall buildings to their right. "These three are the inner ring. Three, five story T-shaped buildings. Each floor can house up to twenty residents, so the max capacity is three hundred. Huge. One of the buildings had a fire. We're going to fix the damage and bring it up to code. Ms. Durkitt says when that's done I'll stay on as a member of the maintenance staff."

Charles looked up at his father. "Where will we live?"

"Ms. Durkitt's going to show us. I think she said building A."

"We're going to live with the old people?"

Richard hugged his son. "It'll be like living with your grandparents. You'll have your own room. You'll like it."

A woman's voice called from behind, "Mr. Fripp?"

***

"Hello, Charlie," said the yellow haired woman in the brown suit.

"Hello," he replied, and he shook her hand firmly, but not too hard. "Please call me Charles."

"All right," she agreed.

Angela Durkitt's office was in a small room to the right of the main entry. A desk with a flatscreen computer filled one corner. A seating area with two stuffed armchairs, a loveseat and a coffee table occupied the rest of the floor space. Generic watercolors and framed credentials covered the walls. Charles noticed a bookshelf to his left and read some of the titles: *Aging Gracefully*, *DSM III*, *The Power to Believe*, and *Futureshock!* Nothing interesting. He turned back to the conversation.

The adults talked about money, the movers' schedule, and Richard's first work week. Charles struggled to remain still, but failed near the very end.

Mrs. Durkitt, noticing Charles' discomfort, smiled at

Richard, and then turned to the boy. "So Charles," she said, "has your father told you much about his job?"

"Yes ma'am," he replied. "He's told me all that he can."

"You know you'll be living here, in the central buildings?"

"Yes ma'am."

"Why don't we go for a walk?"

The trio stepped out into the main hallway and walked down its length.

"This is the dining room," Ms. Durkitt pointed to a large, open room to her left. "Residents can purchase a meal package that allows them to eat here when they wish. You can eat here any time a meal is being served, as long as it's not a private party."

They walked a little further. "This is the pub," she gestured to her right, but did not slow down. "And this is the games room," she pointed to a room ahead. Charles could see several pool tables within. A few wrinkled, gray haired men were playing. "You're welcome to play when you want, although I ask that you do so with respect." Ms. Durkitt turned and faced Charles. Her cheeks and forehead were smooth, but her eyes were serious and fierce. "We want you to be comfortable here, Charles. I want you to be comfortable. But you also have to respect the building and the residents. They pay to live here and use the facilities."

"Yes ma'am," Charles replied.

She took them through a kitchen and outside, into a green space filled with trees and hedges. "This is the meditation garden. Farther down, there's a pool." She faced Charles again, "Like the games inside, you're welcome to use the pool, but it makes noise. I'm sorry to say that many of our residents don't like noise. You're ten, right?"

Charles nodded.

"I don't think it's fair to ask a ten-year-old to be silent. But I can ask you to keep your noise down. The pool is tricky because it echoes."

Ms. Durkitt led them through the garden and into one of the buildings.

"This is your building, Charles. You and your father will live on the third floor."

Charles wasn't impressed. They were in a common room with couches, end tables and lamps, and a coffee table. A bank of three elevators occupied the wall behind one couch. Other than that, there was nothing. Everything looked clean and neat… and worn. The cloths covering the end tables were faded and frayed. The couch cushions were thin and torn. The lamps were chipped. Everything appeared to be used up and ready to be thrown away. Charles shivered.

"Let's go up to your new home."

***

Their home was a two-bedroom apartment. Like the common room, it was clean and neat, but it felt wrong to Charles. Cold came to mind fastest. He explored his room while the adults talked. Light brown wall to wall carpet covered the floor. The walls were an off white that reminded Charles of dusty chalk. The ceiling was a bland popcorn pattern he'd seen in countless hotels and temporary homes. "Will this one last?" he asked himself.

He opened the closet and was surprised by the size. He walked in, turned around, and jumped up and down without hitting anything. His feet stamped on paper. He bent down and picked it up.

DON'T

read the single word at the top of the glossy sheet. A picture of a painted face stared at him from beneath the words. The man's face was orange, with yellow circles around bloodshot eyes.

GO

was printed under the face.

"Go where?" he wondered. "With who?" He took the sheet and went to find an adult.

Mrs. Durkitt stood at the door, preparing to leave. "What is it, Charles?" she asked as he approached.

"Oh," she said, when she saw.

***

They ate in the dining hall. The cook, a thin man named Kian, prepared a special meal of hamburgers and French fries just for Charles.

"How's your day been?" asked Richard.

"Good," said Charles.

Richard wrinkled his brow and smiled. "And?"

Charles sighed and recited the formula, "And I liked seeing my new room, meeting Ms. Durkitt, and hearing about your job."

"And one thing you didn't like?" Richard prompted.

"That paper," Charles answered. "Why didn't Ms. Durkitt say anything?"

"I don't know," Richard answered. "It wasn't anything you did."

They resumed their meals. Charles finished first and asked to be excused.

"In a minute," Richard answered. "We have options. We can stay in one of the outside houses that's got furniture, or we can camp in our apartment. Which do you want?"

"Apartment," Charles answered.

"Thought so."

Charles scooted out of his seat, and Richard restrained him with a gentle touch. "One more. Today's Friday. Our stuff arrives tomorrow, and then on Monday, you're going to start meeting with Dr. Core. She's a therapist that meets with the kids here."

"Like Mr. Wells in Kansas?"

"This is different. You have to meet with her once a month for us to live here."

"That's weird," commented Charles.

"Yes, but it is what it is."

***

That night they spread sleeping bags on the floor and lit the rooms with flashlights. Richard and Charles shared stories from their past, and Charles asked for the story of his mother and sister.

"I met your mother in college," Richard said, as he had many times before. "We dated for six months, and then we decided to get married. I wanted to do it right away, but your mother wanted to wait until we graduated. It's smart to listen to the women in your life. I listened and we waited for a year and a half. We got married in June in Wisconsin. It was a brutally hot summer, but we got married inside so it didn't matter."

"Where?" Charles asked, as he always did.

"At Our Lady of Sorrows in Madison, WI at two in the afternoon. I wasn't Catholic so we didn't have communion."

"We're Catholic now?"

"Yes, we are, and we go to mass every Sunday and on holy days of obligation. Anyway, so we got married in June and your sister Kate was born in April the next year."

"What happened next?" Charles asked.

"We lived and worked and loved each other. You were born when Kate was two and a half. Then mom had some health problems and we couldn't have more kids."

"But you love us very much," Charles stated.

"Right. Then, in the summer of 2010, your mom was driving Kate home from a doctor's appointment when the brakes failed on a fully loaded dump truck, and it crashed into her car."

Once, Charles had said, "And it flattened them like pancakes," at this part and Richard had started crying. Since then, when Richard told the story, Charles said, "and they didn't suffer."

"Right. They love us very much and they want you to go to bed."

"Yes, sir," Charles replied.

Then it was lights out, and Charles dreamed.

Moving In

The movers arrived at eight a.m. Charles noted the lack of tension in father's shoulders, and he relished the bright smile adorning his face.

Charles showed the movers where to put his things and then went down to the garden to get out of the way. He liked the trees and the silence, and the many walking paths twisting among the tall hedges. "I wonder if any of the old folks get lost in here?" he wondered.

He pretended he was a brave knight on a quest to save

the kingdom. He had to find the path to the center, where he would find and defeat the Great Evil One. Lost in thought, he followed path after path and rounded corner after corner, until he nearly ran into another boy. This boy was a little shorter than him, with dark black hair, brown skin, and a surprised expression.

"Hey," the boy said quietly, but in the silence, it sounded like a shout.

"Hi," Charles replied. "Um, I'm Charles."

"I'm Jose," said the boy. "You want to ride bikes? I've got an extra at my house."

"You live here?" asked Charles.

"With my grandparents," Jose explained. "I can't live with my mom. You want to come?"

"Let me tell my dad."

***

Ten minutes later they were opening the garage door at Jose's house. "Pawpaw got two used," he explained. "Him and mawmaw want me to invite people over. They say I need to play with kids my own age."

Charles was confused. "You go to school, right?"

"Yeah," Jose said, "but people are scared of the Meadows. They won't talk to me."

Jose showed Charles two bikes; one chrome, one white, leaning against the wall. Charles took the white while Jose took the chrome. Charles caught a glimpse of a white blur through the window in the kitchen door.

"That's my mawmaw," Jose said. "You can meet her when we come back."

They rode side by side down the curving, empty street.

"What's the Meadows?" Charles asked.

"It's here," Jose said. "This place is in the Meadows."

Charles was confused again. "What?"

"The Meadows is a big rectangle," Jose said. "The Good Friends Manor is in the corner at the bottom. There used to be a city in the middle, and a lake with a camp up near the top."

"Used to be?" Charles asked. "What's there now?"

"All empty and falling apart," Jose answered.

They completed a circuit of the inner ring. "Boring," Jose announced. "Hey, you want to go meet the other kid that lives here?"

"Who?"

"His name's Dylan. He's old."

***

Dylan lived in a house on the outer circle. It was identical to all the other houses, except its paint was a bright and its grass was green. Charles stood in the driveway with the bikes while Jose rang the doorbell. A thin pony tailed woman answered the door. She greeted Jose warmly with a gentle hug, but scowled when he introduced Charles.

"Another child?" she said loudly enough for Charles to hear, but quietly enough that he knew she didn't mean him to. She muttered something else as she began to walk to him. Charles' instincts screamed RUN! but years of polite deference to adults kept him in place.

"When did you get here?" the woman demanded. She stood within arm's reach. She wasn't big, but her lean, muscular frame led Charles to believe she could catch him if he fled.

"Yesterday," he spat. Sweat dripped from his chin onto his shirt. "We're moving in today."

"Bill didn't say," she mused.

She smoothed her hair with her right hand, took a deep breath, and forced a smile. Her eyes remained hard and cold. Charles didn't trust her.

"I am being so rude," she said. Her smile

softened, becoming warmer and more genuine. Gentle light returned to her eyes. "Come inside, it's hot." She introduced herself as Mrs. Patty. "My husband, Mr. Bill, usually tells me when new kids arrive." She gave them Sprites and showed them to Dylan's room.

"I'm so sorry I was rude," she said to Charles. "I'm glad you and Jose are here to visit." She turned, knocked on the door, and called out, "Dylan, honey? You have visitors!"

The door opened, and a tall, blond haired, blue eyed man stepped out. His thick shoulders reminded Charles of pictures of football players, and his red, watery eyes led him to wonder if he'd been sleeping. Or crying.

"Hey Jose," he said, in a flat, low tone, and gave a small wave.

He turned to Charles and extended his hand. "Hi, I'm Dylan."

***

Dylan's room was stocked with all the games and gadgets Charles had ever wanted: a top of the line gaming

PC and a range of consoles coupled to a wall mounted sixty-five-inch flat screen TV; a full set of the fifth edition Dungeons and Dragons books; a wide range of Star Wars figures, both new production and original; and finally, a large DVD library that included a comprehensive selection of Doctor Who episodes, both new and old. The only thing missing was a blazing fast internet connection.

"They don't allow the internet here," Dylan explained.

Charles didn't understand.

"It's true," Jose chimed in. "There's no internet and no cable in the Manor."

"Your dad didn't say?" Dylan asked.

"We just moved in," Charles said.

Dylan and Jose nodded, and they turned their attention to the nearest console. The afternoon passed in a blur of first-person shooter carnage.

***

Richard was upset; Charles had visited another house without calling, and he was out longer than they'd agreed. Even so, Richard smiled when he'd finished scolding. "I'm glad you made friends. Tell me."

Charles told about Jose and Dylan, and most importantly, Dylan's room.

"Huh," Richard grunted, and picked up their plates. "Dylan's the CFO's son." He scraped food into the trash and turned to face Charles. "I don't like that he's older. That can be trouble." He put the plates into the dishwasher. "Still, there aren't many kids here and you need friends. Come on," Richard waved Charles into the living room.

"There's no cable," Charles commented as they sat down on the couch.

"I know," Richard replied. "But there is one channel. Did you watch at Dylan's?"

Charles shook his head, and Richard turned on the flatscreen. An obese man stood before a neon blue background. He wore khaki pants and a plaid sports coat over a white shirt.

"What I have for you today, friends, is opportunity," the man drawled. "It's connection. It's invitation. It's inno-vation. It's…"

The camera zoomed. Drool leaked from the right corner of his puffy, purplish-pink lips. Sweat beaded on his brow. Light reflected from his thick, bulbous, orange framed glasses.

"…the MD 2000!" The screen switched to a shot of a rounded, bulky monitor with a built-in keyboard.

"It has hundred of byte and tens of mega-bits!" The camera panned left to right across the keyboard, stopped, and panned back across the monitor, right to left, as the man intoned, "and it has all the shades of green you've ever dreamed!"

The shot switched back to a full body view of the fat, sweaty man in the mismatched suit.

"All yours for a small investment of…"

The commercial cut to a pixelated graphic of a red sun over a brown background. The words Bright Days were printed in blocky orange text on the bottom of the screen. Your Friends at SFN!!! faded in over the top of the sun.

And then the screen switched back to the fat man, now perched on a stool in front of the computer, stabbing at the keyboard with fat fingers.

"What is this?" Charles asked.

"Bedtime," replied Richard, and he turned off the television.

Building C

"You're going to want to change into some coveralls," Dwon said.

They stood in the kitchenette of the maintenance building drinking coffee, waiting for the shift to start. Dwon's thick brown coveralls were unzipped to the waist, so that Richard could see he wore an undershirt and shorts beneath.

Richard grimaced. "Why do I need coveralls?"

"Craig told me to show you building C. It's nasty in there. We're going in with the full kit: masks, gloves, helmet, and coveralls."

***

Dwon and Richard put a ladder in the bed of the maintenance department pickup and drove over. On the way Dwon explained, "We're going in through the second floor. They keep one window unlocked for access. The first floor's sealed from the outside, but we have total access once we're in." He took a moment to turn right. "But we're not going down to the basement."

Richard let the conversation die, and they unloaded in silence. Dwon pointed out the window, and moments later they stood side by side in the bedroom of unit 212 C. They wore their respirators around their necks. "We only need them on the first floor," Dwon explained.

212 C was unremarkable. Starting at the second floor, Dwon led Richard upward through each floor, stopping for water on the roof.

Sweat streamed down Richard's face and soaked into his clothes under the coveralls. "Why do we need these?" he asked, plucking at the thick, coarse fabric. "All I've seen is minor stuff."

"Wanted to do the first floor last," Dwon panted between gulps of water. "Less time the better."

Richard nodded. "Then let's do it."

The warm, moist air in the stairwell was still and stagnant. Richard smelled mold. They walked steadily and slowly. Richard wanted to prompt Dwon to speed up, but chose not to.

They walked in silence, which was fine for Richard, but unusual for Dwon. In the few days Richard had worked with the man, he'd learned a great deal about his family (separated, three children, all girls) and about his approach to life (non-political, non-religious, loved football, especially the Atlanta Falcons). Today, though,

Dwon was silent, which Richard regarded as an ominous sign.

The temperature dropped and the moisture lifted as they descended below the second floor. Richard thought he felt a breeze, but he chalked this up to imagination. The stairway ended in a thick, double locked door. Tape sealed the seams where it meshed with the doorframe. Dwon pulled the tape away and turned to face Richard. "Ready?" he asked. "No talking from here on," he said as he pulled up his respirator. Richard took the hint and pulled his on, then nodded.

Dwon opened the door just wide enough for himself and squeezed through. The second Richard was through, Dwon smashed the door shut and resealed the seams.

This hallway was different from the others. The ceiling was stained black, and dark specks floated in the air. A strong odor of char penetrated the respirator, and Richard began to choke. Dwon braced him, keeping him upright until the fit ended. After, they walked single file with Dwon leading and Richard following.

They proceeded down the hall into the front lobby. The area was bare save for blackened wisps that floated along the floor, crumpled papers, and flower petals.

Richard pointed at a red petal, and Dwon slashed his hand downward. Dwon motioned for him to follow, but a figure on a drifting scrap caught his eye. Richard stopped, picked up the crumpled sheet, and smoothed it out.

FIRE!

was emblazoned at the top, over a picture of a burning figure. The figure's left arm was extended forward, searching, while the right was curled in around his bowed head.

"What?" Richard thought. He dropped the sheet and picked up another. This one had a red crayon scribble in the center, with the words BLEED SLOWLY typed underneath. Richard discarded this one, and picked up two more.

Dwon snatched the papers from Richard's hand and pulled him to his feet. He gestured impatiently to a nearby hallway. Richard, still intrigued by the oddly illustrated sheets, followed reluctantly.

The air thickened and gained weight as they crossed the hall's threshold. Richard's eyes ached and his ears throbbed. His movements slowed and became awkward, as though he was walking on the bottom of the ocean. A thought bubbled up from deep within, "But where are the sea anemones?" He paused, and more washed in, "Is that me? Who's thinking in my head?" A sharp shove shattered his reverie, and he resumed walking. "Where's my head at?" he thought.

A metallic, bitter taste penetrated the respirator and coated his throat. Richard coughed lightly. Dwon slapped his arm, and directed Richard's attention to damage on the walls, ceiling, and floor. Holes in the drywall exposed blackened studs, torn and shredded wiring, and broken PVC plumbing. Long scratches, four abreast, scored one section of unbroken sheetrock at chest height. Richard examined one scratch and noticed white, translucent particles in the track. "Fingernails?" he wondered.

Dwon pushed him along, and he turned his attention to the ceiling. Wires, light fixtures, and plumbing hung down, creating obstacles. Until this moment, Richard had been walking through them without noticing.

A pile of debris had been swept into a massive pile at the far end of the hall. "How are the residents ever going to get out?" drifted into Richard's head, along with a second of light, nervous laughter. Richard began to choke, and Dwon smacked the back of his head, bringing him back to his senses. He noted the floor sagged and felt spongy in places. "Total loss," he thought. "Needs to be gutted."

Dwon took his left elbow, conducted him around several clumps of dangling wires, and stopped him in front of a smooth, matte gray door.

"Naval," Richard thought. It did not match the rest of the hall. "New." The number 107 was stenciled in large, white numbers on its surface. Dwon pulled his keyring and opened the door. Richard stepped forward, and Dwon pulled him back. Dwon pointed to his eyes with his right hand and then into the room. Then he pointed to his feet and slashed the air.

Richard held onto the doorframe and leaned in. There was a small galley kitchen on his right, a wall on the left, and pitch black straight ahead. Dwon passed him a flashlight. The intensely bright beam revealed a severely damaged living room. Richard could see that the suspended ceiling had been torn away along with any fixtures and plumbing. A few strands of wires dangled down, like postmodern tree roots. The drywall on the sides, while mostly intact, appeared to be charred or stained black. A picture frame hung directly opposite of

Richard's position, but he could discern nothing more than its shape. Lighter rectangles were scattered haphazardly across the remaining space. One of them fluttered. Posters, Richard realized. But of all the significant things to note, Richard focused most on the floor. Or more accurately, the fact it was missing.

A foot-wide rim along the edge was all that remained. Richard shined the light into the ink black depths and… something flickered. "What did I see? What moved? Was it pale?" he would ask himself this and more, much later. But now, Richard turned from the hole and fought nausea. He clawed at Dwon, who drew him into the hallway and slammed the door. Time blurred as they rushed out, into the light where Richard vomited black into a cluster of withered brown weeds.

"What was that?" he asked when he finally could.

Dwon shook his head.

"Why don't they knock it down?"

Dwon shook his head again.

"Okay," Richard stood and stretched. "I get it. But how do we fix that?"

Dwon answered this time, "I don't know. Craig says they have a plan." He held up a hand. "But I tell you what. They will pay. Seriously, tell them you're having dreams and they will pay extra and send you to all kinds of doctors. Craig says they picked us, and they want us to stay."

"Who's they?" Richard asked. The question hung in the air, unanswered.

***

Richard was silent at dinner. Charles, noticing his father's sullen and withdrawn behavior, chewed his lip and worried. "Did you get fired?" he asked, hesitantly.

"I have my job," Richard quipped, rocking forward in his chair when his attention snapped back to the present. He considered sharing everything with Charles, and then thought of the conversation he'd had with Craig and Angela Durkitt on his return from building C.

"I can't talk about it," he said.

Richard stood, and the two cleaned up dinner. "Let's watch T.V." he said.

Charles noted the stern note in his father's voice and chose not to object.

On the screen, a man in a white lab coat and blue scrubs talked with two women in green.

"It's tricky," the man said. "Of the utmost delicacy."

"But doctor," one woman said. "She's just a child."

"But there you're wrong," he replied.

The camera zoomed in as the doctor turned to face the screen with squinting eyes and knotted brow. "You see, there is no child!"

Synthesized music swelled, and TOD SECAIRE! THEOSURGEON! appeared in bold yellow letters over the close up of the man's face. The screen cut to a montage sequence: cars raced down an interstate in heavy traffic, one crashed into a parked car, flipped, and burst into flame. A burning man stumbled down a street with his left arm extended and his right arm covering his head. Medical staff sprinted down a long hall, pushing equipment and pulling objects from their pockets. Charles thought he saw one lab coated man pull a protractor and a woman in blue scrubs draw a steak knife. White uniformed men pulled an empty gurney from a wailing ambulance in front of a large building with cracked and broken windows. Medical staff swarmed, and the gurney now bore the burned figure. The doctor from before, Dr. Secaire, placed a stethoscope against the figure's chest, and gave a thumbs-up to the camera. The title reappeared, and the program cut to commercial.

A little girl with brown hair wearing an orange dress colored with a red crayon on white paper. "Need a lawyer?" a stern male voice asked. "Well, why hire one when you can have three?"

The shot cut to three men standing side by side in a room with striped wallpaper and yellow lighting. The men wore brown suits and orange ties. "Call Frank, Stuckart, and Freisler," said the one in the middle. "We're the ones that care," said the one on the left. "And we'll take care of your family," said the one on the right. FRANK, STUCKART, AND FREISLER FAMILY LAW covered the screen, and the shot switched back to the girl coloring with the red crayon. There were words at the bottom of her coloring sheet now, but the shot cut away before Charles could read them.

"That's enough," Richard whispered. Charles saw that Richard was pale, and that his hands shook so much he fumbled the remote.

"What's wrong?" Charles asked.

"Will you just shut up," Richard hissed, and Charles ran to his room.

Doctor Visit

"How have you been since our last session?" asked Dr. Core. She wore a gray sweater and thick black glasses.

Charles shifted uncomfortably in his seat. "Dad yelled at me," he said.

"All right," Dr. Core said in what Charles called her talking-to-kids-voice. "Does he do that a lot?"

"No," Charles replied. "I told you."

Dr. Core leaned back and waited.

"He doesn't hit me or touch me wrong or any of that other stuff," Charles continued. His cheeks felt hot and he felt tears.

"Then why are you upset?" Light glinted off the Doctor's glasses, and for the brief moment Charles couldn't see her eyes, he feared he was trapped in the room with something else. Something monstrous.

Charles screamed.

***

Richard sat on the edge of Charles' bed. "What's wrong?" he asked the contorted, sheet covered figure. Charles grunted.

Richard lowered his voice. "Please talk to me."

Charles let out a longer, louder groan.

"All right," Richard stated. "The doctor prescribed some medicine. She says it'll help you sleep. Will you take it?"

Charles peeked from beneath the covers. Richard held an orange pill bottle in his right hand, and two white pills in his left. Charles sniffled and extended a hand from within his blanket fort.

"No," said Richard. "You need to sit up."

Charles grunted one final time, and sat upright. Richard passed the meds and produced a glass of water to wash them down.

"We'll talk later," Richard added. "But I want you to know I'm not mad. Nobody's mad."

Charles curled up and slept and dreamt.

***

"You have visitors," called Richard. Charles came to the living room to see Dylan and Jose waiting.

"We heard you were sick," said Dylan. "So I called and asked if you were okay. Your dad says you can go out if you want."

Richard smiled at his son and shrugged. Charles didn't understand. He was having trouble thinking.

"You want to go?" Jose piped. "We can walk or ride bikes."

"Go," Charles repeated.

"Yeah, go," Dylan said. "Outside. In the sun."

Charles understood. "Sun," he said as he nodded.

The yellow sun shone in the clear blue sky. A breeze stirred the grass and ruffled Charles' hair. He smiled.

"Looking good," Dylan commented as he smiled.

"You want to walk or ride?" Jose asked.

The warm sunlight felt good on Charles' face. He felt as though he was waking from a long nightmare. "What happened?" he asked.

"You started screaming and wouldn't stop," Dylan replied. "You were at Dr. Core's office."

"Oh," said Charles. He couldn't remember.

"Hey, walk or ride?" Jose asked again.

Charles mumbled.

"Let's walk then ride," Dylan decided.

The trio walked down the circle. Jose told Charles about a DVD his grandparents had bought. "It's the new Star Wars," Jose reported.

"No man," Dylan said. "It's old. You just don't know," and then he laughed and Jose laughed with him.

"It was like a poster," Charles said, cutting through the laughter. "Like the orange man or the red rite."

Dylan gripped Charles by the shoulder and turned him to face him. "Stop."

"Not here," said Jose.

They guided Charles to Jose's grandparent's house, where they fetched bikes. Dylan rode paw paw's Schwinn, while Charles and Jose rode the white and the chrome.

They rode north, to the edge of the Manor.

The Wall and Beyond

Charles hadn't thought about the wall in weeks, and he'd never been to the north gate. Charles recalled how his father described it:

"The wall is poured concrete, four feet thick and twenty feet tall. It forms a square all the way around the manor, which makes it more than two miles long in total length. It has four gates- north, south, east and west. The eastern and southern gates are always locked. The northern and western are open during the day."

Charles remembered asking, "Why do they lock the gates?"

"That's just how they do things around here."

The gate was large and functional: as tall as the wall and topped with three outward facing rows of barbed wire.

"When did they put the wire on?" Charles asked, confused.

"Always been there," Dylan answered. "But sometimes we don't remember." He pointed at the wall extending away to the right and the left. "It goes all the way around."

Charles wrinkled his forehead and concentrated. The world swam and he wobbled on his bike seat for a moment. Jose stepped closer, mouth drawn into a shallow frown, but he did not reach out.

"I've never seen it," Charles muttered. "It wasn't there before."

Dylan planted both feet on the ground and steadied him with his right hand. "It happens. Don't be scared."

"Can we ride?" Jose asked.

Dylan nodded. "We should." He pointed to a booth outside the gate on the right side of the road. "It's unmanned. We can go."

***

They rode side by side in silence. Dylan rode on the left, Jose on the right, and Charles in the middle. Miles of tall brown weeds stretched away to either side of them. Occasionally, Charles thought he saw rusted metal or a glint of glass in a heap of twisted brush and vine, but then they were past and he wouldn't look back.

"That's it," Dylan said in a warm, encouraging tone. "Ride. Don't look."

They came to a town. Squat one story homes were arranged in curving rows. The yards were brown and unkempt. Some had front windows and boarded up front doors, while others showed broken glass and fractured, rotten wood.

"What happened?" Charles asked.

"Everybody left," Jose answered.

"No one came back," Dylan said.

After the homes came a long, segmented, two story building. A large plastic and metal sign on the front lawn announced that it was the

AUGUST EDUCATION CENTER, SERVING GRADES K-12.

"I went here, before it closed," said Dylan.

Charles didn't know what to say, so he kept silent as he followed Dylan around the side. A complicated maze of towers, ramps, bridges, swings, and slides covered a vast area. The ground had once been covered with wood chips, and they could still be seen in places, but the majority was overgrown with weeds and bushes in varying shades of green and brown.

Dylan led them within, to a three-level tower near the heart of the maze. "Up there," he pointed.

Jose entered without hesitation. Charles held back.

"Come on," Jose waved. "It's safe."

Charles hesitated.

Dylan, who had been standing at Charles' side, now passed within wordlessly, without looking back. Charles was alone. A slight motion in the grass, at the very corner of his vision, startled him. It wasn't the motion that bothered him. It was where it happened. It was how it happened. "The corners," he thought. "It starts in the corners."

Another motion came, this time closer, but also at the very edge, where he could barely see it. "Guys?" he called. No one answered.

A third motion, and air swished against his left cheek. Charles panicked and ran into the tower to find the others.

Cleanup

"What's the plan, Craig?"

Richard and Dwon sat in folding chairs in Craig's office, in front of Craig's paper and trash covered metal desk. Craig ignored the question as he typed on the keyboard of a boxy computer perched on one corner. Richard could not see the monitor from where he sat, but remembered that it had a monochromatic green display.

"Well?" Richard prompted.

Craig looked up. His usually bright, green eyes were bloodshot, and his customarily shiny cheeks were a dull, pale gray. No one commented.

"We're going to clean out Building C," said Craig after a moment of silence.

"You said that," Richard responded. "How?"

This time, Craig replied immediately. "Durkitt and the trustees contracted with some company to bring workers to help out."

"What about us?" Dwon asked.

"We'll be in the middle of it," Craig grinned, showing yellow, stained teeth. Richard was glad he wasn't close enough to smell his breath. "Someone's got to direct them."

"But I don't know what to tell them!" Dwon objected.

"Right," Craig snapped. "I'll take responsibility for C. I need you and Rich to take on the rest. That means finishing the electrical in A and taking care of Mr. Waltham and his plumbing issues in 1979."

Dwon laughed. "That man needs to get his ass checked out."

"True," Craig responded with a grim voice and a subtle smile. "You two are also on the hook for finishing the mowing and trimming. Management cut that funding for this month and the next to afford the help with C."

Richard grunted. "I'll do that. I do a better job anyway."

"You know they have the money, though," Dwon commented. "They're doing this to make a point."

"Probably," Craig agreed. "Last thing: someone needs to be on call. Do it however you want. I'm not coming out of that mess to deal with anything. Go to Durkitt if you have to. Bottom line is if I deal with C, then you deal with everything else, and I mean everything."

Dwon and Richard nodded simultaneously. "You got it boss."

***

Richard was sorting paperwork at Craig's desk when the phone rang. Dwon had agreed to deal with Waltham's problems if Richard would man the phone. And so now Richard picked up the receiver and answered in a gruff voice, "Maintenance on call."

"This is Gladys Kemp in 1928. I don't like the company your boy is keeping."

"What?" Richard said, caught off guard. "How is that your business?"

"Dylan is trouble. People look the other way because he used to be cute and now he's handsome, but I tell you he's trouble."

"Ms. Kemp," Richard interjected. "That's not your business."

Gladys ignored his objection and continued, "That Jose is all right, even if he is Mexican. But Dylan is trouble. Ask him why he doesn't go to school. Ask him why he doesn't play sports anymore."

"It's summer, Ms. Kemp," Richard replied in a stern voice. "And this is gossip. I'm hanging up."

"HE'S BEEN HOME SINCE LAST SEPTEMBER!" Gladys screamed as the receiver clicked into the cradle.

***

Gladys called many more times over the next hour. Richard listened for a minute to each new call, timing his hang ups to the second with his watch. "Don't feed Charlie meat!" she demanded on one. "Meat makes them fat and lazy!" "You've got to wash the whites separate," she whispered another time. "You don't want everything turning pink." And on another she pleaded, "Stay away from that orange man and the red rites."

Richard responded to this one. "Orange man? Red rights?"

"Like an owl," she replied. "And think religious, not civil." Richard considered what he was hearing and hung up.

He took the phone off the hook after one final, intense call.

"Richard?" she'd asked.

"What?" he'd replied absently.

"This is Janice," she'd said, her voice wavering.

A hole opened in Richard's stomach. He could feel his arms and legs getting rubbery. "Stop it, Gladys," he'd warned.

"This is your wife, Janice," she'd continued. "Help me I'm in hell."

Richard threw the receiver and punched the wall. When he was done crying he counted to one hundred, and set the receiver on the desk. There were no messages on voice mail when Dwon reset it six hours later.

***

Charles was out when Richard came home. He noted the silent stillness, and thought, "Like a beast in the jungle, waiting to pounce." He busied himself washing dirty dishes and then found himself standing in the kitchen, looking for something to do.

Richard jumped when the phone's ring shattered the silence. His heart raced and his breaths came quick and shallow, as if he'd been running for a long distance. Counting to ten steadied him enough to answer.

"Yes?" his voice warbled, and he cringed away from the receiver.

"Mr. Fripp?" asked a familiar, female voice.

"Ms. Durkitt?" he asked.

"Yes," she answered. "Craig is missing. The foreman for the cleaning crew needs him. It's your job to find Craig and make sure the foreman's needs are met."

"I'm off shift," Richard answered. "Dwon's on call."

"You're never off," Ms. Durkitt replied. "And I'm asking you and not Mr. Wilson."

Richard felt pressure rising behind his eyes and coming to a point in the center of his forehead. He visualized twin jets of steaming blood spewing from both nostrils while he attempted to moderate his tone. "My son will be coming home soon," he explained. "I need to be here for him."

"I think you'll find this is in Charlie's best interest," she said.

"What does that mean?" Richard snapped, but the line was already dead.

***

Richard found the foreman waiting in the lobby when he stepped out of the elevator. He was a tall, severe looking man with short gray hair.

The foreman fixed Richard with a glassy, emotionless stare and did not offer his hand. "I need a signature," he said, extending a clipboard with an attached paper.

"I'm Richard Fripp," Richard said with carefully measured grace. "We haven't met."

"Yes," the foreman replied. "The signature?" he asked, again holding the clipboard out to Richard.

"What's this for?" asked Richard.

"Affirmation of the covenant that is needed to receive further units."

"Units?" queried Richard. "What does that mean?"

The foreman answered in a sharp sarcastic tone. "Unit indicates men, man hours, tools, and all resources generally needed to complete the task at hand."

Richard focused on the first item in the list. "The signature is for men? What men?"

The foreman's sarcasm receded, replaced with a flat, nearly monotone drone. "Additional units to supplement those currently assigned to your immediate supervision for the purpose of the basement cleansing."

Richard shook his head. "I'm not signing. Follow me, we'll find Craig and he'll sort this out."

***

Charles came home to a silent, still apartment. The stove was cold, and there was nothing waiting in the fridge. "Dad leaves something when he's going to be out," he thought. It occurred to him he hadn't checked the fridge door for messages.

GONE. WORK.

a note on the fridge announced. Charles' stomach lurched. The big, block letter handwriting was not his father's. Richard never wrote such terse notes, and he always added "love you" at the end. He pulled the sheet down and flipped it over to find

DON'T GO

and the Orange Man staring. He dropped the sheet and walked quickly, but did not run, to the front door. Ten, twenty, thirty breaths later, he considered what to do. His father was missing, it was after five, and so the office staff had gone home. He could dial the maintenance on call number, but the phone was in the kitchen.

He thought. The phone was in the kitchen with a harmless sheet of paper. He could wad it up, tear it up, or burn it. He could make the call. He would do this.

But the sheet wasn't there when he went back. "Blew into another room when I went out," he thought. "Slid under the fridge." He picked up the phone and dialed the on call number.

"Charles," an old woman's voice answered. "Are you calling to apologize for your father's manners?"

"Where's dad?" Charles asked, voice wavering and beginning to crack.

"Apples and trees," the woman answered and hung up. Charles stood with the receiver to his ear until the dial tone stopped, and then returned it to the cradle. Another number. He needed another number. A sheet on the wall listed emergency contacts. He called the police. The phone rang and rang, and then cut off. He called three more times with the same results. Then he called the fire department. Then the hospital. All the same. At the very bottom he saw Ms. Durkitt's home number.

She picked up on the first ring, "hello?"

"Help," said Charles.

"Is this Charles?" Ms. Durkitt asked, her voice steady, strong, and slightly stern.

"Yes," Charles replied.

"Your father is completing a job for me. He will

return home soon. Stop calling around like a foolish little boy. Make yourself some dinner and watch television." And she hung up.

＊

Bowl of steaming ramen in hand, Charles sat on the couch and turned on the television.

A sagging woman in a brown plaid sport coat and a matching ankle length skirt sat in a luxurious arm chair. She faced an identical chair, in which was placed a child sized doll. The doll was undressed, and had brown fabric for skin, black buttons for eyes, and an embroidered red line for a mouth. Its rounded, lumpy hands did not reach the end of the armrests, and its feet dangled at least six inches from the floor.

"And why do you feel that way?" the woman asked.

The doll did not answer.

"Fascinating," the woman said. "And what was that you said about the Orange Man? Tell me, have you attended the Red Rite?"

Charles leaned in and turned up the volume.

＊

Craig was nowhere to be found. He wasn't in his

office. He wasn't inspecting any of the recent work. He wasn't at his home on the Manor's outer circle. And now, Richard couldn't find Dwon, either.

"Sign," the foreman prompted.

"My answer isn't changing," Richard answered through his teeth. "No."

They stood outside the door to Craig's office in the maintenance building. "I'm calling Durkitt and then I'm going home."

The foreman remained silent, the forms and pen at the ready on his clipboard.

Richard strode over to the desk he shared with Dwon, snatched up the receiver, and stabbed the pad with his index finger.

"Yes," Angela Durkitt answered.

Richard spat out the details, paying no attention to his tone of voice or choice of words.

"Mind your temper, Mr. Fripp," said Ms. Durkitt. "Sign the papers and go home, if that's your wish."

Richard refused. "No. You do it."

"Very well," Ms. Durkitt said, and then hung up. Richard slammed the receiver down and returned to his truck, without the foreman.

***

The apartment was cold and dark. Richard could hear music from the living room. Was the television on? "Charles?" he called. A muffled something replied. Was it a groan? A grunt? A moan.

Richard hurried to the living room.

A GOOD FRIEND IS SILENT

was printed in large, pixelated yellow letters across an orange background on the screen while elevator music played. The sound came again, quieter yet distinct from the music. Richard turned the flatscreen off.

"Charles?" he called again. A muffled moan came to him from the direction of the bedrooms. Richard charged to Charles' room and threw the door open.

There was a fuzzy lump on the other side of the bed, next to the closet.

"Charles?" Richard whispered as he drew closer.

The moan sounded again. Richard squatted next to the lump and began to untangle a twisted knot of sheets and blankets. He found Charles at the very center, naked, but with underwear pulled over his head and socks stuffed into his mouth. "My boy my boy," Richard chanted as he cleared Charles' mouth. Charles coughed and shook and began to cry.

Richard cradled his son in his arms.

"I am not a doll," rasped Charles.

Course Adjustment

"What is this shit?" asked Dwon as he sifted through a stack of papers.

"Copies," Richard answered. "I found them on Charles' bed when I came home."

Dwon held the sheets in the light of a nearby lamp. "All this shit's blacked out, and the rest is too blurry. I can't tell what it says." He shuffled them. "These pictures are creepy, man." He handed one to Richard and pointed to a washed out, grainy, black and white photo of children standing at attention in a playground. They wore slacks or skirts with backpacks and stood with their hands at their sides. Every face was blacked out from the mouth up.

"They're all like that," Richard responded.

"Ah!" Dwon recoiled, backing into the cushion on the couch, nearly spilling his beer.

Richard reached over and retrieved the paper from him, calm and serene.

"This was on the refrigerator," he said, holding up the sheet.

NOT HOME
ALL GONE

was hand printed on the front in orange crayon, and a large orange handprint covered the back.

"It feels wet," said Dwon.

"Like moist skin," Richard agreed. "Hold them long enough and they all do."

Dwon was drinking beer. Richard held an open can, but had not taken a sip. They sat on the couch in Richard's apartment while Charles slept in his bedroom, sedated. The flatscreen was on, but turned to a channel filled with white static.

"Why are you still here?" asked Dwon.

"Two reasons," Richard replied. "One: Charles is too sick to move. He tried to bite me when I gave him his meds. I held him until he started crying, and only then would he take the pills.

"Two: Charles could get worse or die. You can read the blurry lines on those sheets if you use a magnifying glass. Kids that leave here get worse. Many die. The only way to get him back is to fix whatever's causing it.

"And three: Durkitt made it clear that the trustees will sue for breach of contract if I leave before my two years are up. I'll have to pay back the signing bonuses and thousands more. They'll ruin us."

"You said two," Dwon commented.

"Yes, I did."

They sat in silence. Dwon drank his beer and then drank Richard's.

Dwon spoke. "My wife wants to come back."

Richard sat forward.

"She says I'm making excuses when I say 'don't come.' She doesn't believe what I say. Somebody's been sending her letters about all the financial and medical benefits they get if she moves here. She says she talked to some man, told her she don't have to live with me. She just has to stay inside the manor."

Dwon stared at the floor, and then finished his thought. "With the kids. She gonna bring my girls here and I can't stop her."

Richard stood up.

***

The sun was shining. The birds were singing. Richard was driving, and Dwon had a hangover.

"1928," Richard said, shifting the truck into park. "We're here." Dwon groaned.

Richard spoke without looking over, "Stay here. I'll get you if I need." It was understood that he would not.

Richard retrieved a bag and a claw hammer from the toolbox in the truck bed and then walked up the concrete path. A shriveled woman with wispy white hair answered the door.

"Gladys Kemp?" he asked. "Your house wiring needs a thorough check. We've been notified that sub-standard material was used in its construction."

Richard pushed past her and walked into the living room.

"You can't come in!" Gladys protested. "There are rules!"

Richard drew a stack of papers from the bag, thrust them in the woman's direction, and dropped them at her feet when she refused to take them. "It's all there," he said. "Everything typed and witnessed. I have every right to be here. Remember, this is the Manor's house. You just live here."

Gladys drew back and hissed. "What's this about?"

Richard set the bag down and approached a nearby wall. "I'm going to open the walls to have a look," he said. "Or we could talk about my son."

Gladys drew near, eyes flashing through slitted eyelids. "Am I your son's keeper?" she queried, jabbing her right index finger for emphasis.

Richard pushed her back with his left hand and lifted the hammer in his right. "You tell me," he said, and he launched the clawed end forward, tearing a long, jagged hole in the immaculate white wall.

"Stop" Gladys shrieked. "You'll fry yerself!"

"Hm," Richard grunted. He withdrew the hammer and began to rip at the hole with his gloved hands, tearing out chunks of drywall and tossing them away.

"You can't, you can't!" cried Gladys.

Richard paused in the midst of the destruction to point at a cluster of framed photos. "Grandkids?" Richard asked.

"Stop, stop," Glady's sobbed.

Richard hefted the hammer. "It's too bad you didn't put these away."

"STOP!" she whined at the top of her voice. "Just stop."

Richard stopped. "And my son?"

The words rushed out of her mouth quickly, quietly. "I don't remember it all. I don't remember much at all now."

"What?" Richard raised the hammer. "What don't you remember?"

She held her hands before her, pleading. "I lose days. I wake up and don't know where I been. People say I talk with them, call them, curse them. I don't remember a thing."

Richard dropped the hammer. Tension bled from his shoulders. "I can't do this," he told her.

Standing two feet apart from one another next to the ruined wall, the father and the old woman cried.

***

They drank coffee in the nook at the very end of the kitchen. A large bay window gave Richard a view of a tall wooden fence around the brown grass of her postage stamp sized back yard.

"I moved in six years ago," she said. "There were more people here then. And there were people living in the town north of here. There were children, and the school was still open."

Richard said nothing.

"I came because my husband died," she explained. "I lost his benefits and our savings weren't enough. Back then, this place was a bargain: good facility and services for just a little money. The catch was that you had to sign everything over. You could leave if you wanted, but they'd take a chunk."

"Right," Richard said. "They get you with a contract."

"And more than that," she said. "You see now how they get the youth. They eat them up till there's nothing left."

Richard grimaced. Gladys continued.

"But it's more than that. They get everybody." She paused, stared into her coffee, and looked up again. "How many people live here? In the Manor?"

"We're under capacity," Richard answered automatically. "Right around three hundred residents, out of a total capacity for five hundred."

"Wrong," Gladys answered, her voice shrill and harsh. "We got way less than that. Count the residents you met. Count the staff. Count yourself and your family."

"That's a handful," Richard said, tilting his head and furrowing his brow.

Gladys remained silent. They drank coffee.

"Tell me about the posters," Richard prompted. "Tell me about the Orange Man."

Gladys's eyes widened, her face paled, and she scooted back. "You must want trouble, "she whispered after a moment.

"Well?"

"Different people make the posters," she said. Her eyes remained dilated, but some color returned to her face. "Most recent was Albert in C."

"Lived in 107," Richard said.

"Gone for years," Gladys replied. "But he made the most recent batch. Hideous things." Gladys tapped her coffee cup. "A better question is who puts em out?"

"And?"

"Got no names. Just shapes. You can see em if you look out of the corner of your eye. You can feel em moving behind you. Under you. Around you. But never in front."

"People?"

"Maybe."

Richard took his coffee to the sink and poured it out. "Thanks," he said. "I'll be by to patch your wall later."

Gladys turned from his gaze and stared out of the window. "I used to be a grandma. I got a son and daughters. They used to visit and bring my grandkids. My daughter won't talk to me. My son said I'm not his mother. He don't know me. I don't see my grandbabies."

Richard returned to the truck and woke Dwon, who was sleeping fitfully.

***

Charles shuffled through a long white space. The air felt cold and dry on his cheeks. His eyes ached.

"How..." he began to think. More would not come. His thoughts were rotting logs mired in the stagnant swamp of his mind. He shuffled.

His left hand brushed something cold. A silver circle on a swinging rectangle. "Doorknob. Door," the words came to him, unbidden. Charles leaned, and the door opened inward. He noticed numbers on its surface as he stumbled past.

"Where..." he tried to think again, and gave up.

Charles focused on taking one step after another. Blue

veins stood out on the milk pale flesh of his numbed bare feet.

"Hey," a familiar voice called.

"Uh," Charles responded, looking up. A thick string of drool leaked from the left side of his mouth.

He stood before a window in an empty square room.

"What are you doing?" the voice asked. "You shouldn't be out."

Charles was confused. The voice wasn't coming from the window. Where was it? Who was it? He shuffled, and pressed his nose against the window's cold glass.

"You're going to hurt yourself," said the voice. A hand gently touched his right shoulder. Charles flinched, and for a moment he saw a brown doll sitting in a soft chair. "I am not a doll," he said.

"Of course not," the voice responded. The hand on his shoulder pulled him back and around.

Charles stood face to face with Dylan.

***

Richard locked the front door and returned to the truck. Dwon was leaning against the passenger side door, squinting in the harsh light of the late afternoon sun.

"And?" Dwon asked.

"Empty," Richard answered. "Everything's clean and ready for move in, but the dust shows nobody's been inside for months or maybe years."

"That's the fifth?"

"No," Richard replied. "You slept. This is the twentieth."

Dwon rubbed his forehead. "Twenty empty?"

"It's more than that," Richard said. "I drove us around the complex before I started. I don't see cars, and the curtains are drawn on most of the houses. I think ninety percent of them are empty."

"How'd that happen?" Dwon demanded.

"I don't know. I think it's always been like this."

***

Dwon made a sandwich when they returned to the maintenance building.

"How can you eat?" Richard asked.

"Skipped lunch," Dwon explained. "What are you going to do next?"

"Talk to Durkitt, maybe." Richard poured himself a cup of cold coffee. "Or maybe… have you ever seen Jose's grandparents? Or met Dylan's mom and dad?"

Dwon finished his sandwich. "I saw both Dylan's parents some time back. Dylan's mom Patty is with Durkitt all the time. I saw her driving yesterday. Who's Jose?"

"You're kidding," Richard said. "Jose's one of Charles' friends. His grandparents live on the middle ring in 2135."

Dwon held up his hands. "Never heard of him. You want to check?"

"Not now," Richard said. "I should go home."

Patty was waiting in the hall outside when Richard came home.

"Dylan's gone," she said.

Absent

Jose watched the man and woman rush to the truck. He listened to their stressed breathing, and noticed their pinched, pale expressions. He stood motionless astride his bike in the shadows, a hidden observer of their muted, managed grief. The man slammed the driver's side door and started the truck. The woman was already belted in and grasped the handle on the roof above the passenger seat. Jose visualized her white knuckles in his mind. The man reversed without looking and sped away. Jose took a moment to ponder the scene and then decided to go home.

Jose pedaled down a starkly lit, totally empty street to his grandparent's. The garage door was closed. Jose considered dropping the bike and going in, but recalled how the veins had bulged from his grandpa's slick, red forehead and how the spittle had sprayed from his chapped, dry lips. For his grandpa's health, Jose opened the garage and put the bike away.

Inside, Jose called a greeting to his grandparents and opened the refrigerator. He couldn't remember eating, but as he looked inside he realized that he didn't feel hungry. The fridge was cold and empty. Bare shelves reflected the interior light. Someone had cleaned it thoroughly.

Jose shrugged, closed the door, and entered the living room. "Hey mawmaw," he said to a shadow in the corner. Onward, down the hall, Jose passed the bathroom and the guest bedroom. He paused for a moment outside the master bedroom. Should he bother grandpa? He opened the door and offered a soft, respectful greeting. He paid no attention to the total lack of furnishing, the undisturbed dust on the floor, or the absolute silence that swallowed his words. He did notice a figure, but he didn't look too closely at its blurred outline, its posture, or the sign it showed with its left hand.

Jose closed the door and crossed the hallway to his bedroom.

SFN

Charles sat on a dusty chair in a square room. Thick glass doors opened to the outside, and a single solid wood door blocked the path that lead further within. A glass window to the right of the wood door enclosed a desk space. "Receptionist," Charles thought. "Is this a doctor's office?" Chairs and benches filled the floor space and lined the walls. End tables in the corners held stacks of magazines. Charles reached out and picked one up, and noticed for the first time that the space was very dark. Too dark to read, in fact.

"Where am I?" he asked out loud. Startled and near panic, Charles began to check himself. He had ten fingers, two hands, two arms, two legs, and he could feel his toes wriggling in his slippers. His teeth felt slimy and his lips were dry and chapped. His eyes seemed to be working and his thoughts felt clean and clear. "Where have I been?" he asked.

He stood and continued his self-examination. He wore the thin green cotton scrubs he used as pajamas, and his favorite pair of slippers were on his feet. "When did I get dressed?" he asked. "Did someone dress me?"

Charles rolled the magazine into a tube. Brandishing it before himself as a weapon, he began to creep around the room. Just enough light came in through the double doors to allow him to avoid stumbling and falling. He approached the double doors. Through them, he could see a large parking lot. Weeds pushed up through large cracks in the asphalt, and several tall light posts had toppled. A car was parked in the corner on the other side of the lot, but its hood was up and its tires were flat.

Charles pushed the panic bar to release the door. It did not budge. He pushed hard. No movement. Charles screamed for help, and slapped at the door with his magazine, but no one answered. Silence dominated.

Charles turned and considered the other door. The reception area was dark. Charles felt certain the door led deep into windowless hallways. That wouldn't be safe. Couldn't be safe. But Charles saw no other option. He didn't know how long he'd been here. "Who will find me?" Charles shuddered and crossed the room to the wooden door.

***

COME AND SEE!
MARAH PLAINS DEVELOPMENT!
OVER 100 UNITS READY FOR OCCUPANCY!
MOVE IN TODAY!

Charles read from a twenty-seven-year-old glossy promotional sheet. A tiny pinpoint of fire burned in the very center of Charles' forehead, just above where his eyebrows met. His stomach swirled and roiled around a deep, cold, emptiness. What was all this? He looked around the room again.

He'd stumbled inside, blundering down the pitch-black hallway. The overhead lights had come up by themselves with a click, and when he'd finally been able to see, he'd found himself surrounded by fully stocked cardboard displays. Each one represented a different time span: one display far to his left dated from 1995. Two displays to his right covered the years 2001-2005. He'd gravitated to the most elaborate. Where all of the others were the size of a tri-fold poster and fit three to a table, this one was more than two tables lengths wide, and another two tables deep. The sheet in his hand, the man sized posters, and arching overhead banners all declared

NEW FOR 1989!
A REVOLUTION IN COMMUNITY!

Two large dark screens occupied carts at eye level at the back of the display. Charles felt a deep aching need to see the video they'd shown, and at the same time fought a strong urge to vomit. He turned from the display and studied the floor until the nausea passed.

Charles wandered around the room, picking up literature. Happy grandparents played with smiling children while beaming, beatific parents watched. Industrious men and women worked hard under the golden sun. People of all races and creeds stood shoulder to shoulder. If you believed the pamphlets, then this place would be paradise. "But it isn't," Charles thought. "What did they really build?"

He took a closer look at several of the sheets.

Developed by Gary Thomas and the NTRA Group was printed on each, sometimes at the bottom, sometimes at the top. Charles wondered, and continued wandering. He came back out into the hallway, and saw the lights were on here too.

Charles flinched. The orange man and a host of other bizarre figures, blown up to theater marquee size, stared out at him from both sides of the hall. The DONT GO message was familiar, while others were totally new. Charles' stomach cramped and for a moment he thought he was going to soil his pajamas. Shame flushed his cheeks as he fought his body. Slowly, when his bowels settled, Charles stared at his feet and put one foot in front of the other. "Just get out," he thought. "Survive."

The Tower

"What is this?" Richard asked. They stood side by side at the top of the three-story tower in the center of August Education Center's massive playground structure. He pointed to a five-foot diameter circular design at his feet. A medallion had been etched into the industrial plastic with a sharp tool, and color- paint, ink, or something else- had been worked into the lines, adding contrast and definition.

Richard stepped within and stared at the figure in the center. It had the body of a man, but a tree with ten branches grew where the head should be. Its arms and legs ended in intricate root systems. Each branch of the head-tree bore one five-pointed star. The figure's body was colored in orange, the star fruited tree was colored in red, and the root hands and feet were brown. Black symbols were clustered into groups and arranged in circles around the figure in three concentric rings. A braided design formed a fourth decorative ring around the outermost edge. The braids looked wrong to Richard: soft. Moist.

"This is where Dylan came," Patty explained. "This is where he brought Charles."

Richard nodded curtly. His hands balled into tight fists. "Yes, but. What. Is. This?" He asked through clenched teeth. He nodded again towards the medallion on the tower floor.

Patty shrugged. "I don't know," she said.

"Why are we here?" Richard growled, raising his eyes to meet hers only to find she'd turned away.

"Our sons are missing."

"This is where Dylan comes," Patty repeated. "I thought he might be here."

Richard pointed at the floor. "This," he gestured, "Doesn't come from kids. Are those letters? That figure! What was your son doing up here?"

Patty shrugged again. She'd been very upset at the manor: yelling one minute, crying the next. She'd wanted action and she'd wanted it now. No time to wait for police- she knew where to go. But now she seemed calm. Her body hung loose, relaxed, and Richard thought her words displayed an alarming lack of concern.

"He came here," she repeated. "I don't know why. I followed him once, just to see where he was going. I followed far behind. I don't think he saw me."

"Where is he now?" Richard demanded. Sweat beaded on his forehead. "I want my son!"

"Of course," Patty replied, placid. She turned to face Richard, and the emptiness in her cold blue eyes drove an icicle of fear through his heart and down into his gut.

"What is wrong with you?" Richard whispered. A terrible idea blossomed within his mind. "I'm so stupid," he thought. Out loud, he cursed Patty and said, "You knew."

A single tear leaked from the corner of Patty's right eye. She turned away. Richard descended the ladder to the ground.

End of Line

The hallway's dirt brown carpet was worn smooth in the middle, and shiny concrete showed through long tears. Charles did not bend to touch it; he imagined that it felt like the green scouring pads he and his father used to clean dishes after dinner.

Charles stared at his feet and did not look at the posters on either side. Steadily and faithfully, he placed one foot in front of the other. When he came close to being overwhelmed, he paused to take a breathing break. "In, out," he chanted. "In, out."

Charles noted that the floor gradually sloped downward, but it was so slight that someone who wasn't staring wouldn't notice. Charles walked for what felt like an eternity, and the hallway kept leading him lower and lower. "The wrong way," he thought. "But where else can I go?"

Then it ended. Charles looked up. A beige door with a frosted glass window in its upper half barred his way. Light shone through the glass, but he couldn't see inside. A brass plaque the size of a postcard to the right of the door frame read SFN. There were no posters to the right or left, but there was a potted plant: a shoulder-high, big leafed, healthy green, and recently watered. "Who's been watering you?" Charles asked.

The plant's healthiness unnerved him, and he realized how clean the building had been. Every inch of every room was dust free: no trash, no accumulation of anything that wasn't meant to be there. "Everything in its right place," Charles whispered. "Does that include me?" For a brief moment, he had an overwhelming sense of being moved and placed, like a chess piece on a checkered board. Charles wanted to run, but instead he reached out and opened the door.

Searching

Richard drove aimlessly through the decaying development of Marah Plains. Rows of dark, boarded up houses crept by in the deepening twilight. Had he been down this road before? How many times? He took a left at the next intersection and continued.

He drove alone. Patty was still at the top of the playground tower as far as he knew. He could do this alone. He would.

The road curved to the right, and he crossed over a creek on a small bridge. Trees lined both sides of the road, narrowing his line of sight. He crept forward at 20 miles an hour. "Thorough," he thought. "Find him."

Then the trees ended. The road curved to the left and ended in a four way stop. And there, kitty-corner from the red sign, stood the Marah Plains Municipal Center. Richard paid no attention to the cracked and weed infested asphalt parking lot. He didn't care about the abandoned car resting on its rims with its hood up in the corner. He didn't see the toppled light posts.

He saw the bikes: two of them, identical to the ones he'd seen Jose and Charles pedaling one morning a few weeks ago. He gunned the motor and shot through the intersection. Metal ground on concrete as the truck bounced over the curb and dug trenches through the grass. Tires squealed as Richard stopped the truck just shy of the main doors. His breaths came quick and even as he fetched a hammer and crowbar from the truck bed toolbox. Nothing was going to stop him. He was going to get his son, dammit.

SFN

Charles stood at one end of a long, rectangular room with a low popcorn ceiling. Seashell shaped wall sconces emitted a warm, buttery light, and the heated air was slightly moist and bitter. Charles smacked his lips and took a step.

Thick orange carpet squished under his feet. Tall square racks filled with vinyl records covered the wall to his left. A long low floral print couch occupied the wall to his right. A sturdy wood desk sat in the center of the far end of the room. There was a wood door with a frosted window in its upper half behind and to the left of the desk. "I guess that's where I'm going," Charles thought.

He walked forward, no longer focusing on his feet. The room was long and boring. Air hissed from a vent. The bitter smell increased. Charles pulled out a record from the racks. A bearded man wearing a cream three-piece suit lounged on the LP cover. *Dennis Rawls Sings the Hits* was scrawled across the top in gold script. "Never heard of you," Charles whispered as he put it back. He browsed through a few more, confirming that they were all equally obscure and dated.

Charles' stomach grumbled. How long had it been since he'd eaten? And just like that, he realized he'd relaxed. He felt no fear. Why was that? He scratched his head as he walked to the desk.

A legal pad of narrow ruled paper and a #2 pencil were the only things on the scarred and dented desktop. Neat legible writing covered the top page, all done by the same hand. Charles turned it around and read:

THE GOD KILLERS
Amit, Justin, Smiley, Gary

At the top. Well below this, in the very center was written:

> **How long wilt thou forget me, O Lord? For ever? How long wilt thou hide thy face from me? Wherefore came I forth out of the womb to see labor and sorrow, that my days should be consumed with shame? For the thing which I greatly feared is come upon me, and that which I was afraid of is come unto me. I was not in safety, neither had I rest, neither was I quiet; yet trouble came.**

And then at the very bottom was written:

> **If yellow is the color of muted violence,**
> **Then orange is the color of suppressed anxiety.**

"What is this?" Charles asked. He knew the Bible, but he'd never seen that verse before.

A distant boom followed by an echoing cascade of shattering glass snapped him back to the present. It sounded miles away.

Should he run? Charles was scared. Which way should he go? He took a moment, and then proceeded forward, through the unlocked door.

Searching

Richard didn't know where he was. He didn't care. The building interior was a maze of interconnected rooms and hallways, all smothered in a thick, inky darkness. The power was out and daylight was still hours away. He lit his path with a flashlight he'd found in the first office he'd entered. He'd still had his crowbar and hammer back then. Now he carried the light in his left and the hammer in his right.

Richard rushed up and down stairways, around corners, and through doorways. He thought he'd seen it all. All, that is, except for Charles. He called his son's name until his throat hurt, and heard nothing more than dripping water and creaking wood in reply. Where was he? Charles' bike was outside. He had to be here. But where? Richard pressed on, entering a curving hallway with a low ceiling. He swung his flashlight side to side, trying to decide which way to go, paying no attention to the posters hung on the walls at regular intervals.

Richard walked up the hall, passing closed doors on his left and right, finally stopping before a door labeled LOBBY ENTRANCE. The door swung open with a touch, and Richard entered a square room. His feet slid as he stepped on a magazine. Richard saw a receptionist window to his left, and glass double doors directly ahead.

"Charles!" he called. The carpet and cushioned chairs absorbed the noise. "Charles?" he asked, quieter, this time with despair. Where could he go from here?

Richard walked to the double doors and looked out as he considered his options. He could return to his truck. In fact, he could see it if he pushed his face to the glass and looked to his right. Or... the bikes lay five feet away, in a straight line from where he stood. Why hadn't he noticed that before? Charles must be behind him somewhere. He'd gone the wrong way in the hall! Richard ran through the lobby door, into the hallway. He shined the light ahead, and kept his hammer at his side. Richard considered the doors he passed along the way. They were all closed. Richard stopped to check one: locked. Hope fluttered in his heart. "I'm coming, Charles, I'm coming."

A GOOD FRIEND IS SILENT

was embossed across an exposed metal beam on the low ceiling. He couldn't get a feel for the size of the room; it was too cluttered. Racks of glowing equipment formed walls in front and on both sides. Erratically spaced doorways lead from here to who knows where. A console encrusted with buttons and

topped with monitors showing white static occupied the center. Poor lighting coupled with thick cables snaking across the floor made walking difficult. Charles cautiously worked his way around one side of the console towards a doorway in the back.

Something pale caught his eye as he rounded the console: a hand. Charles recoiled, but did not run. It was a normal hand, man sized, clean and with clipped fingernails. It was laying palm up, and it was attached to an arm. The hand twitched and the fingers flexed as Charles watched. Slowly, he peeked around the corner.

Dylan. It was Dylan, with his back propped against the console, his feet out before him, and his right hand lying to one side. His head sagged to the left. He was drooling on himself.

"Dylan," Charles called. "Dylan."

Dylan stirred, but did not wake. Charles stepped closer and shook his shoulder. Dylan sputtered and raised his chin, but he did not open his eyes. He wiped his mouth with his left hand.

"Wake up," said Charles.

Dylan grunted and wiped his eyes with both hands, then opened them. "Not again," he growled.

"What?" Charles asked.

Dylan looked up, showing Charles raw red eyes. "I'm sorry," said Dylan.

"Sorry for what?"

Dylan cleared his throat and began to stand. "Everything. We should leave before he gets here."

Charles stepped back to give Dylan space.

"Look," Dylan appeared thoughtful, as if he were about to say more, but then he shook his head and said,

"Just follow me."

Dylan walked and Charles followed, not because he trusted Dylan, but because he was afraid. How would he get out if Dylan disappeared? Dylan walked steadily and without hesitation, effortlessly threading his way through the snaking cables without tripping. Charles struggled to keep up, to the point that he watched little more than his own feet and Dylan's back. They passed through doorways and down halls. All the rooms looked the same to Charles, with cables on the floor, gadgets in the walls, and banks of consoles scattered around.

"What is all this?" he asked once when Dylan waited for him.

"Later," Dylan answered.

More doorways and halls followed, and then they stopped at a large metal door. This one was different from the others Charles had seen: its surface was smooth gray metal, with multiple thick locks clustered around a stout, bulbous doorknob. Dylan whistled seven times and tapped thrice on the door with his left middle finger. The locks clicked in unison and Dylan opened.

Charles followed Dylan into a dusty white room. The ceiling merged seamlessly with the walls, and the floor was tiled in white dollar bill sized rectangles. Long white coats hung on hooks to either side. Another gray door lay straight ahead. This one had no visible locks. Charles started as the door shut behind them with a solid thump and loud clicks. Dylan proceeded through the opposite door with Charles close behind.

The next room was wide, open, and bright white. Thigh high counters and eye level cabinets were spaced evenly throughout the room. Occasionally a counter and cabinet were joined together into one unit by a glass partition with two fist sized holes in its front. Each section of counter top included at least one metal sink with a goose neck faucet. Light blazed from strips set into the ceiling. The green of Charles' pajamas stood out amidst the room's stark sterility. Charles wiped a finger along a nearby surface and it came back gray. Maybe the room wasn't as clean as he'd thought.

Charles looked up to see Dylan halfway across the room, stamping his right foot repetitively while waiting. "We've got to move," Dylan hissed when Charles drew near, but he pulled away before Charles could say anything. Again, Charles followed. They exited the dusty white room and entered a short hallway with a plastic gray floor. The hallway formed a plus sign where it crossed another. Dylan turned right, walked up the hallway and stopped before a door.

The lights blinked, and Charles heard a door slam. "Thought he'd catch us by now," Dylan said. He turned his gaze towards Charles, who shrunk back a step. Dylan's face was pale and his expression was flat, but his eyes blazed. With what, Charles couldn't tell. Fury? Excitement? Charles wondered if Dylan meant to hurt him.

"Look," Dylan began, "I don't think we'll have time, but I'll tell you what I can if we get through this next place. You have to stay quiet in here, okay?" Charles wanted to say he'd been quiet and patient up to now, but chose to nod instead.

"Here we go," Dylan said, and he pulled Charles through the door into a damp, humid room. This was like the first white room, in that the ceiling melded with the walls and the floors were covered in dollar bill sized tiles. But unlike that room, the floor sloped inward toward a circular drain, and low benches ran along the walls in front of small lockers. There was an exit door at the far end of the room, and an open arch to the right. Charles saw toilets and showers through the arch as they passed. Dylan and Charles paused before exiting.

The door opened into a room with a pool. But it was a pool unlike any Charles had ever seen. It was long and oval shaped, with blue and white tile squares along the rim. Wires draped down from the ceiling and bunched into knotted piles on the bottom. The pool had been drained of water some time ago- it appeared bone dry to Charles' eye- but it wasn't empty. Shadows flitted and stirred within the rats' nest of wires. Charles stared until Dylan dragged him away by the left elbow. Even then Charles did not stop watching; the shadows were entrancing. A light flickered somewhere, but he couldn't see. If only he could get a little closer. And some of those shadows seemed soft and rounded. Not threatening at all. He wondered what they'd feel like... Warm or cold? He noticed a long mirror along the wall on the opposite end of the pool as the door closed on the room. "It's where they watch from," he thought.

Confrontations

Richard crashed through a door at the end of a hall, and then he was... standing at the foot of an enormous tree with ten branches. Richard saw fruit sprouting from each branch, but the produce on the lower branches looked funny, like... his mind recoiled. They were men, hanging by their necks. But were they alive or dead? As Richard watched with horrified detachment, the lower figures twitched and writhed in agony.

The figure lowest and closest to him was eerily familiar. Richard wiped his eyes, and against his better judgment, looked closer. The man, hanging maybe twenty feet above Richard's head, wore a generic gray uniform and black shoes. Richard wore that uniform at... at... his detachment shattered and he remembered: the Good Friends Manor. And now he knew the contorted, purple face. This was Craig, his boss. Richard threw himself at the trunk and tried to climb, but he couldn't get a grip. Once, twice, and on the third try he fell hard on his back, out of breath with bleeding hands.

"Who is he to you?" a voice asked. Richard turned to face a young, dark complexioned boy. He knew the kid, but wouldn't take time away from rescuing Craig to remember his name.

Richard, crouching low with his hands at his side, prepared to lunge. "Who is he to you?" the boy asked again, interrupting.

"Um.. he's... my boss," Richard sputtered.

"Oh, "the boy replied. Richard felt the space change,

and he stood in a brightly lit hallway. Craig slumped against the wall to Richard's right, gasping and drooling. The deep purple of his face was fading, replaced by healthy pink.

Richard turned to face the boy. Thoughts sloshed through the swamp of Richard's mind. He breathed deeply, and connected the face with a name. "Jose. You're Jose," he said.

The boy paid no attention. "Why?" asked the boy.

Richard remembered something important. "Charles," he said. "I came for Charles."

"Yes," Jose answered. And then he was gone, and Richard was alone in the hallway with Craig.

Blood oozed from Craig's eyes and ears as he struggled to stand. "Why... down here?" he gasped when Richard began to help him up.

"Down?" Richard asked. "We're north of the manor."

"No," Craig replied. "...under C."

Richard shook his head. "Let's find you a chair." They shuffled down the hall. Richard scanned both sides for a door, but saw nothing.

"Home," Craig grunted. "Go home. To kid."

"I lost him," Richard replied. "Came here to find him."

"Here?" Craig straightened and pushed Richard away. "Shit."

Richard didn't know what to say, so Craig spoke. "I'll manage. Go." Richard stepped away and Craig slumped against the wall. Richard hefted his flashlight in his right hand and walked away. He absentmindedly realized he'd lost the hammer. "Where did it go?" he wondered.

Reunions

Charles sat on a couch in a kidney shaped room, where smooth walls blended into a slick ceiling. A soothing pastoral scene of a shepherd leading a flock of sheep through a verdant green pasture illuminated the walls. The scene extended across the ceiling with clouds, birds of all shapes and sizes, and the golden yellow sun in position at mid-day. Even the room's couches and carpeting matched the pasture's swaying green grass. Charles noted all these details as he thought over Dylan's departing words:

They said they wanted to talk to god face to face, like Moses or Adam, and call him to account. "I want to meet my maker and tell him he fucked up" is the way one said it, and they all agreed.

Charles had stared, glassy eyed yet deeply focused on what was being shared.

They succeeded. A few were satisfied, but most wanted more. Now they wanted to touch god and "make him move for a change." So they tried that next.

Charles nodded.

That succeeded. More were satisfied, but a small remainder wanted more: to hurt god. "The way we've been hurt. Make him suffer as we've suffered." They succeeded. In the end four remained, and they shared one goal: to kill. To permanently erase his presence from the reality he'd created. They were split, though, on what to do when they succeeded. Two wanted to replace him, while the other two wanted to eradicate the possibility of a highest. "All Indians, no chiefs," was one of their slogans.

"What happened next?" Charles had asked.

Then there was us. Think about it: Who's closest to the heart of God?

Dylan stood next to the door they'd just passed through. "I have to meet him face to face. I want you to count to 100 and walk out. If things go right, your father will catch up with you soon. If that happens, tell your dad to go north. There's a chapel by a lake where you'll be safe." And then Dylan walked through the door and out of Charles' life.

"...99, 100," Charles finished counting and stood. He noticed there were doors other than the two exits in this oddly shaped room. Charles stopped to examine one on his way out. A sheep was painted across it, and the door itself meshed with the wall so well that a person could easily overlook it if they missed the shiny silver doorknob. The sheep painted on the door wore a nametag, which read, "Ella." Hand on doorknob, Charles paused and looked at the other sheep in the scene. They, too, were painted over hidden doors, and like this one, each wore a nametag. Charles turned and knob and pulled the door open smoothly and quietly.

The room was a smooth, windowless oval. The walls were a gentle shade of pink, with flowers and butterflies painted all over. The carpeting was a plush dark purple. A frilly pink canopied bed occupied the center of the room, with a white dresser to one side, and stuffed animals scattered throughout. Charles sneezed. Dust flooded his eyes and nose, pushing him to make a hasty retreat. "Why is that room dusty and this one clean?" Charles asked as he made his way to the exit.

The room shook. It was a small, brief shake, but a shake nonetheless. Charles sprinted to the exit.

***

Richard crossed a trash strewn, overgrown gravel lot. Damp, thigh high weeds swished against his thighs, leaving wet smudges on his canvas work pants. The humid air smelled of mold and fruity rot. Richard wiped his nose and fought a sneeze. Something in the air did not agree with him.

"Charles?" he called. After leaving Craig, he'd walked down a few hallways and come to a thick, panic bar equipped door marked "exit." He knew that Jose had given him something- what, he didn't know, but he hoped it was a path to Charles. So now he wandered across an overgrown gravel parking lot calling Charles' name.

And there, at the far edge of the lot, he saw movement. Richard hustled, water splashing and trash crunching. He vaulted a neon orange mesh fence at the lot's edge and sunk knee deep into a ditch of muddy water. Undeterred, Richard followed a faint flicker across a muddy, grassy field and into a grove of trees. What he followed he could not say. Later, he would say he saw a bird, and simply knew he had to catch it.

And so it was that Richard entered the grove and came to a concrete building at its very heart. It was a smooth cube, one and a half times taller than a man. There was a handleless dark gray metal door on one side that opened over a concrete pad. Richard stood on the pad for a moment and slapped at swarming mosquitoes while wondering how to get inside. A thump and a series of hollow echoes sounded from behind the door, and then it shuddered in its frame. Slowly, slowly it opened. Richard stepped back to give the door room to swing.

Charles stepped through. Richard snatched him up in his arms. "I searched for you," said Richard.

"I was with Dylan," said Charles. Richard, carrying Charles in his arms, walked out of the grove on the far side, away from the gravel lot and the place that had nearly consumed them.

"We can't go home," he told Charles.

"North," Charles said. "I know a place."

Richard set Charles down, and together they walked away, towards a chapel on the side of the lake in the north, looking for safety.

Language of Birds.

Hiring. Independent contractor for high priority job. Ideal candidate is physically, mentally, and spiritually fit. Must pass stringent drug screening. No credentials, certification, or prior experience necessary. Job involves significant risk. Generous compensation and benefits.

Interview

They met in the conference room of a prestigious law firm in a downtown Milwaukee high rise. The Foundation representative wore a crisp black suit and introduced himself as, "Edward Black."

Hunter wore a clean polo shirt and wrinkled khakis. Sweat darkened his pits and stained his collar. Not all of it was due to the heat. Hunter introduced himself by first name only and then accepted a handkerchief from "Edward," to wipe his face. They sat alone at a long table that could comfortably seat twenty. A manila folder stuffed full of paper occupied the space between them.

"You're our ideal candidate," said Edward. "We hope you accept."

"Really?" Hunter asked, confused. "Because I don't understand. There's so much money."

Edward frowned. "Why is that an issue?"

"Money comes with strings. What are you paying me to overlook?"

Edward flashed a hard, cold smile and sat forward in his seat. "Excuses," he replied. "What's the real problem?"

Hunter shifted in his seat and scratched his balding scalp. "I'm not qualified. I don't know anything about assessing."

"Your experience in the ministry is enough," Edward replied smoothly. "And we're not concerned about the physical condition as much as the spiritual."

Hunter sat back in his chair. "I don't do that anymore," he said. "I don't believe.

"Which makes you our ideal candidate," said Edward.

***

"Why'd you take the job?" asked Angela Durkitt. They stood in the parking lot of a run-down hotel in northern Illinois. The sun was setting. Hunter shivered, even though the temperature was in the 80s.

"I'm out of options," Hunter replied. "They'll 'repair my reputation.'"

"What does that mean?" she asked.

"A ton of money, I guess." He paused and looked away, towards the sun. "I talked with my wife for the first time in over a year," he said quietly, almost whispering. "She let me talk to our oldest."

"So what," Angela brayed, trampling the delicate moment, "did they ask you to do?"

"They want me to go to a park and assess three buildings."

Angela waited.

"They gave me your number. Told me to talk to you."

"Right," she said. "Let's eat."

Angela led Hunter to the hotel restaurant, which turned out to be cleaner on the inside than it appeared from outside. They sat in a corner booth, and the waitress brought them menus.

"The food's good," said Angela. "It's a traditional greasy spoon, the kind you don't see much anymore." She paused and then added, "I'm buying."

The waitress returned. Hunter ordered an omelet with

a side of French fries. Angela ordered a cheeseburger and coffee.

"I was the administrator," Angela began. "But now I'm not."

Hunter frowned. "Of the park?" he asked.

Angela chuckled. "No, of the Good Friends Manor, an elder care facility in the southeast corner of the Meadows."

"Okay," said Hunter.

"The Foundation dismissed me, but they still pay."

"To do what?" Hunter asked.

Angela smiled mirthlessly. "How long will the job take?"

"They said a couple days."

"Where will you stay?" she asked.

"There's a church next to the park that has water and electric. They gave me keys."

"Food? Supplies?" she asked

"All provided," he answered. "They bought me a jeep and gave me the title."

Their food came. Hunter ate some fries and then picked up where he left off. "They gave me a laptop, too. They say there's no wifi or cell reception, but this laptop can connect at three pm each day. I have to update them daily."

"What do you need from me?"

"You tell me," Hunter said. "They told me to meet you. Here I am."

"Right," she said, and smiled again. "They used to call me with a name, and tell me to 'equip the candidate.' Now I don't even get a post-it. Just a monthly deposit in the bank and a phone call from some new moron." Angela sipped her coffee. "No offense."

"None taken."

"Good man," said Angela. "I used to give a little speech and then hand out a list of rules. Sometimes they came back. One day, one of them called me. He said it didn't make a difference. None of it did. I stopped."

This time, Hunter waited.

"That one never came back," she said.

Hunter and Angela ate in silence. When the meal was finished and Angela had paid, she began preparing to leave.

"What can you tell me," Hunter asked, "since I'm here."

Angela stood. "Don't go," she answered. "Just like the poster says."

Report

From: hunter@ntra.org
To: foundation@ntra.org
Re: Report

Arrived and scouted the park. Took longer to get here than I expected. The roads are in decent shape- clear of debris, no wash outs, and no big potholes. The raw distance is misreported in the directions. The layout of the Mara Plains community is complex. Roads loop back on themselves or end in cul-de-sacs when they should go all the way through. The land is a big open plain. Why didn't they build in a grid?

I found the park at approximately six pm. I had some time before the sun set since it's summer. The park is circular. Maybe 100 feet in diameter. I said I'm bad at judging distances at my interview, and you hired me anyway.

There's a smaller circular concrete dais in the center of the park; it's maybe ten feet in diameter. Twelve benches are spaced around the park perimeter like the hour markings on a clock.

So there's one at the one o' clock, another at the two o' clock, and so on. A waist high pillar stands a foot or two behind each bench. Most of the pillars are empty, but the twelve o' clock pillar and the eight o' clock pillars still have bronze metal rockets. The twelve o' clock rocket is labeled Apollo Four, while the eight o' clock is labeled Gemini Three.

The dais at the very center comes up about a quarter inch from the ground, and has a circular bronze plaque in the very center. The date 1-27-67 and the names Grissom, White, and Chaffee are etched into the surface. I have no idea what it means. There are three curved benches positioned evenly around the dais.

Neatly trimmed grass covers the rest of the park. Somebody's been doing a good job at cutting it. There's no playground equipment, grills, or anything else. The church is to the right of the park, past the three o' clock bench. The library is straight forward, past the twelve o' clock, and the clinic is to the left, past the eight o' clock.

I found a man resting on the three o' clock bench. He says his name is Dwon Wilson. He was dressed in a stained khaki work uniform. How should I deal with him? Is he homeless? He asked to come with me, so I let him into the church.

Grace Fellowship is mostly empty. There's some empty desks and a couch in the office. There are two rows of pews, ten on each side for a total of twenty, facing a platform with a table/ altar in the sanctuary. There are no Bibles or hymnals in the pews and no paraments on the altar. The kitchen's the exception. It's stocked with everything anyone could need to make a meal: pots, pans, plates, silverware, and all the rest. The only things missing are the ingredients. The fridges and freezers were clean, empty, and cold, and the stovetops and ovens all heat up.

Dwon and I didn't talk much; he didn't tell me anything other than his name and I didn't tell him about my job. He found a bathroom with a shower in the basement. Dwon washed while I made some dinner. We ate and then separated to find places to sleep. Before he went away, Dwon said, "Don't bother keeping watch. Won't make a difference."

Library

Hunter and Dwon ate breakfast in silence at the counter in the kitchen. Hunter assumed this was the last he'd see of him. "I'll go my way, he'll go his," he thought.

He was surprised when Dwon followed him to the lobby.

"I'd like to come," he said when Hunter gave him a questioning look. "Is that all right?"

Hunter saw no reason to refuse. He shrugged and they walked the short distance to the library side by side.

The Marah Plains Library was a flat roofed two story brick rectangle with non-opening arrow slit windows. "Designed for air conditioning," Hunter thought. "It's going to be a sauna inside."

The library main entrance was on the north end of the building, away from the park. Hunter paid little attention to the cracked and empty parking lot or the curving black asphalt road to which it connected. He was focused on getting inside, and at that moment enjoying no success. "Locked," he spat as he kicked at the stout metal double doors.

"Hey," Dwon said. "Chill. I know a way."

Dwon led Hunter around the side to the left, to an unmarked metal service door. Dwon waited, then rapped a pattern: one-two, one, one-two. "Go ahead," he said to Hunter.

Hunter stepped forward, twisted the knob, and opened

the door without effort. "What was that knocking about?" he asked, before proceeding inside.

Dwon shook his head. Hunter considered leaving, and then walked in.

The door opened into a stairwell. Stairs descended from the first-floor landing to a basement level and another set ascended to the second floor. Straight ahead a metal door labeled with a big white 1 led into the library itself. The air in the stairwell was slightly cool with a light trace of moisture, to Hunter's surprise. "Air conditioned," he thought. He pushed through the first-floor door with Dwon following close behind.

DON'T GO

was printed in large, white letters on an orange poster hanging on a support pillar five feet from the door.

"That's intense," Hunter said. Rows of empty floor to ceiling shelves to the right and left walled them in. Books were piled in columns on the floor along the wide main aisle that ran the length of the building. Cardboard boxes, full, empty and halfway, were scattered randomly amidst the columns of books.

"I'm not sure what my job is," Hunter said to Dwon. "I don't get what they want me to do."

Dwon hesitated before replying, "You'll know it when you see it, and if you don't you get paid anyway."

Hunter shrugged. "Let's go upstairs."

One flight up, the cleaning job was mostly complete. The shelves were clean and bare and there were only a handful of filled boxes near the stairs. Hunter sighed. "Basement, then."

Dwon lingered. "You know you're not the first, right?"

"What's that?" Hunter asked.

Dwon stood in the center of the main aisle. A brilliant ray of morning light shone from behind, illuminating the edges of his shoulders and arms, casting everything else into shadow. For a brief moment, Hunter felt as though he was talking to a dark void or bottomless pit.

"Others have been here before you," Dwon said.

"Right," Hunter confirmed. "Durkitt said." After a moment he added, "Why do you care?"

"Cause," Dwon said and stopped. The light passed, and Hunter could see Dwon's face again.

Dwon continued, "I just." Dwon's forehead wrinkled and he spoke slowly. "I don't want trouble."

"Huh," Hunter grunted. "It's too late for that."

Answer

From: foundation@ntra.org
To: hunter@ntra.org
Re: Report

Virgil Grissom, Edward White II, and Roger Chaffee burned to death in a fire during a launch rehearsal on January 27, 1967. The mission was designated Apollo 1 on April 24, 1967. The launch pad was abandoned and still stands, unused since then, at Cape Kennedy Air Force Station in Florida.

Dwon Wilson is a former maintenance worker at Good Friends Manor. We want you to hire him as an assistant. Tell him we will renew our previous agreement.

Library

The basement door was sealed with silver duct tape. Hunter stared at the giant white B stenciled on the door and doubted. "What do you think?" he asked Dwon.

"They don't pay me enough," Dwon replied.

"Well," Hunter muttered, and then began pulling the tape away in one, long strip. "I think we should replace it when we're done. I'm sure we'll find some tape in a supply closet or over in that clinic."

Hunter opened the door. A fine cloud of particles puffed out, coating him head to toe. The world blurred and narrowed down to a tiny white dot as he hacked and spat, struggling to breathe. Saliva drooled from his lips in long strands and hot, viscous snot bubbled from his nostrils. He remembered

head down, legs up, in cold water. Four hands touched him: two held his ankles and two pulled at his swim trunks. His hands slapped the water but could not stop them. He was going to

Air rushed in and the world grew. Watery blurs gave way to clear sight, and he noticed his surroundings. Hunter knelt on a rust brown carpet in an oval room. A sign on the ceiling to his left read TEENS and a similarly positioned sign to his right read CHILDREN. The teen section was filled with rows of fully stocked, chest high, bookshelves. A circular conversation pit anchored the children's section. Hunter estimated that the pit was one foot deep and ten feet wide. A low bookshelf ran around the edge of the pit. Most of the children's books were scattered across the pit floor.

Hunter spit grit. "What was that about?" he asked,

turning to Dwon, finding no one there. "Dwon?" he called, but no one answered. "Well," he said. Hunter's head throbbed and he felt nauseous. "Have I been poisoned?" he asked as he wobbled into the children's area. He saw a door opposite the one he'd entered. This one was rusty and thick, and most interesting, had no doorknob or handle. "Opens from the other side," Hunter thought.

He reached down and mindlessly picked up a thin, flimsy booklet. The pages trembled as he held them in his right. Little black and silver spots bubbled in his line of sight, and his head felt light. "I need to sit," he thought as he focused on the book in his hand.

YOUR SILENT FRIENDS

read the title in bold, white letters above two faceless children with perfect hair and white clothing who were making shushing signs with their index fingers.

Hunter looked up and saw
a life sized poster of a nude man painted orange from head to toe. He was bald, and there was yellow around his eyes and on his lips.

Hunter vomited.

Report

From: hunter@ntra.org
To: foundation@ntra.org
Re: Report

I was exposed to something in the library basement. Stomach upset with associated problems over the past four hours. I thought it was asbestos- still concerned it might be- but Dwon tells me all the construction in Mara Plains was completed in the 90s after it was banned. He says my problem is allergies and imagination. I hope that's it, but in any case, I want a full medical workup when I come out and I expect you to cover it.

You can see that we explored the library. It was mostly empty, except for the basement which appeared to be untouched. When did they clear it out, by the way? And why? The library looked like it had been abandoned in the middle of emptying or stocking.

And what's with all the creepy posters and children's books?

Church

Hunter and Dwon ate dinner at the kitchen counter inside Grace Fellowship.

"I remembered something," Hunter said. "Today, in the basement."

Dwon continued eating and did not look up.

"I went to a pool when I was ten years old. I was playing by myself when two older boys decided to show off for some girls. One held me by the ankles while the other tried to pull my trunks down. My feet were up in the air and my head was down in the water. They didn't notice I was drowning."

Dwon paused, a spoonful of beans halfway to his mouth. "Lifeguard?" he asked.

"It was a pool behind a gym where my parents were members. A swim-at-your-own-risk kind of place."

"Oh," quipped Dwon, and he resumed eating.

"Some other boys saw what was happening and tried to stop them. There was a fight. The gym owner came out and cleared the pool. Got me up on the deck and I started puking water. I passed out during the fight for maybe a second or two. It felt like years. While I was out, I saw."

"You saw what?" Dwon asked.

"I saw walls in a desert. Water flowed from the right side and ran down to a city. The people drank from the water and they needed nothing else."

"You saw that when you were drowning in a pool?"

"And more," Hunter continued. "There was a light in the walls. I heard it speak and I saw its words."

"You saw words?" Dwon asked.

"I remembered the pool while I was choking," Hunter said. "I couldn't find you, and I needed help. Then I saw water."

Report

From: hunter@ntra.org
To: foundation@ntra.org
Re: Report

Are there pools here, in Mara Plains? Big pools. Deep pools. Filled with salt water.

Story

Dwon said, "There was a professor from Texas. He taught remedial English at some junior college, but he really wanted to teach Shakespeare. His students could barely handle Doctor Suess, so he never did.

This professor also taught remedial history. That class required a weekend-long road trip. The professor would take his students to some historical place and have them takes notes during the trip.

When they got back, they had to write a paper and make a presentation that would make up half of their final grade. The trip was a big deal.

The professor liked hidden history. He looked for important places everybody forgot. He liked them even better if people forgot on purpose. The road trip always went to places like that. One year they visited abandoned missile silos in Kansas. Another year they went to closed insane asylums in Arkansas.

On the last road trip, he came back without his students. Eleven kids: six girls and five boys between eighteen and twenty-two. All gone. His bosses at the college made him write out a plan any time he went on one of the trips. Every year before this one the professor recorded everything and called in regularly during the time away. This time, there was nothing. No one knew about the trip. One of the bosses said it was canceled. When they asked him, all the professor would say was, "she called me Balaam."

Park

They met at the dais in the park just after breakfast, next to the inscribed plate.

The sun was still low on the horizon, and the air felt cold and damp. Hunter wished he'd worn a jacket.

"I'll take you into the clinic," Dwon said. "I'll show you the first and second floor. You could skip the second. There's nothing up there."

Hunter scratched his chin and thought. Dwon continued.

"I stayed there for a while after I left the manor." Dwon stared down at his feet. "I didn't like it." He shifted his weight from side to side, and looked up, over Hunter's right shoulder. Hunter considered turning to see where Dwon was looking.

"There's a bunch of stuff on the first floor. Back in some offices. Somebody else lived there. I've got some ideas about who, but you should make up your own mind."

"You said first and second floor," Hunter noted. "Is there a basement?"

Dwon shuddered. "Yeah, there's a basement."

Answer

From: foundation@ntra.org
To: hunter@ntra.org
Re: Report

We will pay $1000 per sample of printed media brought out of the Meadows. There are no outdoor or above ground pools in the Meadows.

Report

From: hunter@ntra.org
To: foundation@ntra.org
Re: Report

I scouted the first and second floor of the clinic with Dwon's assistance. He was with me the entire time. He took me through an unlocked service entrance on the side, similar to how we entered the library. Unlike the library, we went straight up to the second floor and worked our way down. The clinic is an L-shaped building. The second floor is mostly waiting rooms, nurse's stations, and exam rooms, with a little bit of office space mixed in. It's empty up there. It looks like someone swept and mopped before leaving. The tile floors are still shiny. Dwon showed me where he slept in the corner of one of the exam rooms. I pressed him for details but he either doesn't know or won't say. I feel very comfortable with Dwon and at the same time recognize that I know very little about him. He won't tell me anything about his past, other than that he did maintenance at the Good Friends Manor. He wore a wedding ring until I asked him about it; he took it off and refused to talk to me for an hour.

The first floor is mostly offices, labs, and storage. The lab equipment is gone. You can see the empty spaces where the x-rays and heavy equipment used to be. Everything else is still there: desks, chairs, phones, obsolete computers, and filing cabinets filled with patient records. Someone else has been there. There were piles of records next to a desk in one room. Several of the records were open on the desktop, and there were pencils, pens, and a pad of paper nearby upon which someone had been taking notes. One room over, there were twelve sleeping bags laid out in a row in an empty conference room. At first glance, they all appeared to have been used recently: they were wrinkled and ruffled, and a few were open. But when I looked closer, I could see a thick layer of dust that showed they'd been there a while. The room also contained a pile of equally dusty packs and duffel bags. We didn't touch them, but we could see toiletry bags and rolled up clothes inside the open ones.

Dwon took me down a hall to a break room kitchenette where the counters were overflowing with spoiled food. There were no insects: no ants, roaches, or flies, in spite of all the rotten food. This was an old mess; dust had settled over everything, and even turned the thick stains on the counter a light shade of gray. It stunk, so we moved on.

Our last stop for the day was a supply closet a few doors down from the break room. It was windowless, with duct work and heavy pipes on one side, shelving for supplies on the other, and an area for hanging mops in the front corner. It was long and narrow, and cleaning supplies had been piled in the back. There was a white circle on the floor near the front. The circle was wide enough for one person to stand in, and the line that formed the circle was about a quarter inch thick. It appeared to be made of powder. I reached out to touch, and Dwon stopped me. I don't know why and I didn't ask.

Three notebooks were stacked in its center. I began to step inside and Dwon stopped me again. I reached over and picked up the notebooks, making sure not to touch the line. Dwon made no attempt to intervene.

I've looked through them, and they appear to be one journal and two notebooks of data. It's too much to copy here, but I will include excerpts that are of interest.

Answer

From: foundation@ntra.org
To: hunter@ntra.org
Re: Report

We wish to emphasize our interest in all printed material that can be brought out of the Meadows. We will make retrieving all such material financially lucrative.

In the interest of backing up valuable information, please reproduce as much of the journal and data as possible within the body of the daily reports.

Journal

Ram, Mandy, Serge, and myself, interviewed the widow at her home. She was short and wrinkled, and I assume that her thin curly hair was supposed to look styled. It didn't.

She served us water, tea or "pop" and then sat down in a fluffy orange armchair in the corner of her living room.

She insisted on calling me Balaam, even after I introduced myself for the third time.

"I know who you are," she said while looking me in the eyes. "I'm making sure you know."

Church

Hunter drew a figure on a piece of paper when they finished dinner.

$$\text{מִים}$$

"This is what I saw. When I was drowning."

Dwon shrugged. "Not English."

"Right," Hunter agreed. "It's the Hebrew word for water."

Hunter waited, and when Dwon did not reply, he began to lecture.

"Humanity had a complicated relationship with water in ancient times," he said. "In those days, oceans and lakes were places where men could not go. They might be able to float on the surface a short way, but even that was dangerous. At times it seemed that the water was attempting to destroy them on the dry land with flooding from below and rain from above.

"It's no wonder, then, that water came to represent chaos. The god of the Hebrew Scriptures controlled the water and brought order from within it. That's the significance of separating the waters from the land in the creation account. Internal evidence from within Genesis indicates that the ancient Israelites thought of reality as a dome. Their god had banished the chaos from the dome but yet kept it visible. Every time the Israelites looked up at the blue sky, they saw chaos waiting to rush in and destroy them. Their god allowed this to happen at Noah's Great Flood. So water represented chaos, disorder, destruction, and death.

"But water was also life. Consider Moses and the Israelites in the wilderness. They were dying of thirst in the desert after their god delivered them from slavery in Egypt. Their god gave them water from the rock by delegating power to Moses, an ordinary man. In the end, Moses was punished for misusing that authority. Oh, and consider that the Israelites had to pass through water to reach freedom, and that the false god Pharaoh was unable to control the water and drowned.

Hunter paused to take a deep breath and then continued.

"And then, in the New Testament, a carpenter's son from Nazareth began teaching that he was the son of god and that he could give living water so people would never thirst again. This man-god demonstrated his power by controlling storms and even walking on water! Also note that modern Christians utilize a ritual cleansing with water, commonly called baptism, to mark an essential rite of passage. Most Christian baptism rituals explicitly state that the baptized person passes from death into life. There are other practices, too, like the asperges at the start of some Catholic masses, where the priest sprinkles the people with water and says, "I saw water proceeding out of the Temple, and all they to whom that water came were healed." So water and healing. Light and life. Christianity is full of that imagery. But at the same time, when the water imagery pops up there's talk of death and destruction. You can't have one without the other. It is the chaos from which life is drawn.

Story

Dwon said, "I'm married. Or I was married. Or maybe I will be married. And there are three girls. My children. My girls. My wife sent me a letter when I still worked at the Good Friends Manor. She said she was coming back and bringing the girls with her. We were separated then, but not divorced. We had talked about it but we hadn't decided.

"And then the Manor was closed and I couldn't stay. I slept in fields under trees. I tried living in a house in Mara Plains, but that didn't work out. I found the clinic and slept in the corner of a room on the second floor.

"I was always meeting people like you. At first I asked what year it was. They all said something different. One blond kid said it was March 1983. A brown woman said December 1998. This Latino guy said it was summer, but there was snow falling. They came and went.

"I looked for my wife and my girls all the time. I don't think I found them but I don't know for sure. Like I don't remember when they closed the Manor. All I know is I was standing in the road in front of the north gate. The gate was locked and rusted, and there were weeds growing through cracks in the asphalt.

"I keep looking but I don't find them."

Park

Hunter and Dwon stood in the center of the park, facing each other. Hunter stood on the left side of the plaque commemorating the deceased astronauts while Dwon stood on the right, and the sun was rising over them.

"Are you coming with me?" Hunter asked.

"I'm coming in the building," Dwon answered. "But not the basement."

"Will you be there when I come back?"

"I'll wait until it gets dark," said Dwon. "I'll come back every day during the light, for three days. On the fourth day I'm leaving."

"Four days?" Hunter asked.

Data

The Meadows. Rectangle of wilderness and disused farmland under development in northwest Illinois. Project is financed by a group of investors incorporated under the name NTRA. Scope and intention of the project are unknown. Sites of note within the Meadows include:

Mara Plains. An intentional community in the center of the rectangle. Construction began in 1989. Residential neighborhoods were begun in 1991 and most were completed by 1993. Mara Plains can house upwards of 20,000 residents and was intended to be an experimental mixed generation community, where the elderly were housed outside of nursing homes next to younger couples of child bearing years. Mara Plains was intended to be self-sufficient, with its own essential services (police, fire, utilities) and even its own television station. Plans to build a hospital were drawn up but never executed.

Silent Friends Manor. Located in the south eastern corner of the Meadows. A community for seniors. Independent housing is arranged in two concentric rings around a full care nursing facility. The Manor houses up to 1000 residents.

Brown Lake. Located in the northwestern corner of the Meadows. A rustic lakeside vacation resort. Facilities include twelve open plan barrack style cabins, tennis courts, a centrally located cafeteria, a multi-use activity center, and a non-denominational multi-faith chapel.

Report

From: hunter@ntra.org
To: foundation@ntra.org
Re: Report

I went down to the clinic basement today. Dwon waited for me at the top of the basement stairs, which is the only way in or out of the basement that I could find. It feels like they go down two or more stories, and they're so narrow and poorly lit I started to panic before I reached the bottom. I am very thankful that the solid metal door at the bottom was unlocked. There's no way the equipment in the basement came down those stairs, which means there's another entrance somewhere. You're going to have to hire someone else to find it.

The door opened into a space that was half office, half lab. Chest high walls and floor to ceiling glass windows divided the office space into cubes and rectangles. The lab was an open floor plan filled with fully equipped countertops: gas hookups complete with burners, sinks with gooseneck taps, high voltage electric plug ins, and dusty electronics. Most of the computers were more recent than the gear I saw upstairs, but it was still out of date. Ex: The desktops were chunky all-in-one combos that I haven't seen since the nineties.

There was no paper in the office or the lab. Not one sheet of any size, blank or otherwise. There were a lot of locked doors on the office side, which I'm guessing lead to more offices.

I found one unlocked door on the lab side. I went through and found what seemed to be a kid's dorm. The right side of the hall was painted blue and the left side was painted pink. There were six doors on either side for a total of twelve. Each door had a first name printed in script in the center at eye level.

I looked into one girl room and one boy room. They looked like they'd been customized for each child. The boy's room had a Disney theme, with reproductions of Carl Barks-era Donald Duck, Uncle Scrooge, and the three nephews on the walls and a thick blue carpet on the floor. There was a recessed closet containing pale blue ankle length gowns with the name Douglas stitched on the breast, many pairs of disposable slippers, and a bucket of toiletry items. A small bookshelf in the corner contained leather bound compilations of Barks and Rosa Disney comics. The twin bed frame was made of solid metal covered with a thick plastic finish. It was so heavy

I couldn't budge it even a quarter inch. The mattress on the frame was made with Disney sheets, and a Donald Duck plush doll rested on the pillow. Everything in the room was covered in a thick undisturbed layer of dust. No one had been there in a long time.

The girl's room had a horse theme and purple carpet The closet, bookshelf, and bed were in the same location as the boy's, although the books were all about horses and the gowns were pink and labeled with the name Julie.

I found a door marked THEATER at the end of the hall but I could not go through it. A plastic covered NOW SHOWING sign to the right of the door listed "The Language of Birds" as the film for the week. The air thickened as I drew close, and there was a moment when I couldn't breathe just before I reached the THEATER door. I came back up as fast as possible. Dwon says I was gone ten minutes, but I thought I was there for hours.

Journal

Ram and I sat on a stiff loveseat to the widow's right. Serge and Mandy occupied a gray sofa to her left. Serge operated a digital video camera. Mandy sat at the ready with a pad of paper and a pencil. Ram held a digital audio recorder.

I began to introduce the group again and explain the scope of our project, but the widow cut me off.

"Do shush, Balaam," she said. "I know what you want." Then she smiled at me and said, "These students don't know who you are, do they?"

Church

Dwon presented Hunter with a key. "I found this in a closet downstairs," he said.

Hunter stared at Dwon's hand and did not take the key. "I don't believe you," he said.

Dwon nodded. "Okay. Come on." He waved for Hunter to follow.

Downstairs, they crowded in to a small utility closet. Dirty gray overalls hung from a hook to the left, mops leaned against the wall to the right, and a small box marked "keys" hung at eye level straight ahead.

"There," Dwon said, pointing to the box.

Hunter took the key from Dwon and examined it. "But why here? In a church?"

Dwon shrugged. "Like I would know. Maybe they stayed here while they cleaned out that clinic and the library. You ever thought about why we sleep here instead of there?"

They stood in silence for a moment. "Why do you talk so much about God and the Bible if you don't believe?" Dwon asked.

"Where'd that come from?" Hunter asked.

Dwon stared and waited.

"I never heard any voices," Hunter said, to end the discomfort. "The Bible says Adam, Noah, Jacob, Moses, Abraham, all the prophets, and even the apostles talked with God the way we talk to each other. It's not internal dialogue or mental prayer. They talked. God answered. I've never experienced anything like that. It became clear to me that no one does if they're healthy. So either the Bible was written by the mentally ill, or it's an expression of premodern wish fulfillment. I won't lie anymore. Like the man said, "faith is believing what you know ain't true.""

***

"Drowning," Hunter said.

"Bad way to die," Dwon replied without looking up. He was reading a book he'd found in the closet.

"I think about it," Hunter said. "That time in the pool.

I remember what it felt like under water, with my mouth fractions of an inch from air and life. But I couldn't reach. I was going to die, cold and alone."

Dwon nodded and turned a page.

"I'm scared," Hunter said. "All day, every day. I can't stop."

Dwon marked the page and closed the book. "Yeah. Me too."

"How long have we been here?" asked Hunter.

Dwon shrugged.

Data

Three sayings:

1. Do not call up that which you cannot put down.

2. Terriblis este, Locus iste.

3. As below so above.

Answer

From: foundation@ntra.org
To: hunter@ntra.org
Re: Report

How are you sleeping, Hunter? When you sleep, what do you dream?

Journal

The widow took offense when I tried to redirect her. She smiled sarcastically and said, "I see you don't care, Balaam. But maybe your students do." She turned away and asked them, "Should I continue?"

Mandy, who is usually quiet and unobtrusive, raised her hand and asked "Why do you call him Balaam?" The widow ignored her and resumed talking.

"Just after two in the morning on Thursday, three of those white coats crashed a van into some parked cars in the front lot of the clinic. The clinic is a twenty-four-hour band-aid center. They patch you up and send you on. If you really need a doctor, you're better off anywhere else.

"The van's driver died. They never figured out how. They couldn't even tell if it was a man or woman at first. Poor thing just melted at the wheel. The other two got out and walked into the ambulance bay. There was a deputy on duty and he was running to help when one exploded. Sprayed everything in a hundred-yard radius with a big, wet boom. The pieces of bone they found were soft like rubber. And there was too much of everything. Too much blood. Too much flesh. Too many eyes.

"The last one walked into the clinic and attacked a

nurse with his bare hands and teeth. Harlan Boyce, the on
-call doctor, said he was trying to eat her. Harlan hit him
in the head with a fire extinguisher but he didn't stop.
Then the deputy came and shot that white coat five times.
Knocked the poor devil down but he survived. The nurse
survived too, but she lost an ear.

"Which brings us to today. Nothing at all has
happened since then. No one has gone in. No one has
come out. My husband Johnson died five months, three
days, and twenty hours ago. I'll be honest with you. I
don't care anymore. I'm not sure that I ever did. So
Balaam, you can have your followers.

"And you," she pointed at each one of the students
and fixed each one with an icy stare, "need to read your
Bibles."

Data- The Language of Birds.

Concept: Pre-modern cultures believed that birds
communicated in a divine language. Ex: Christianity's
Holy Spirit is often depicted as a bird. The concept
probably began with animistic beliefs wherein the sky
and celestial bodies were worshiped as deities. Birds
could enter the divine realm to commune with the gods
and then return to earth. If one could learn this language,

then one could cut out the intermediaries and talk directly to the gods.

Film: A mythic 1970s production. The legends surrounding it agree: 1) It was shown once. 2) The director was named Preston Rosewater. 3) The film harms its audience. The film community dismissed its existence until last year when a ten second clip was posted online.

The clip: Ten seconds of pixelated video posted under anonymous user names. Most of the names used the word "incarnated" with a string of numbers. Ex: InCarnateD2083748294. The video was totally obscured, but the audio was clear. Those who listened could not describe it after. Many listeners attempted self-harm. Several were permanently committed. One died. Streaming sites took the clip down as fast as it went up. It enjoyed a longer life on the Torrents, but even there users stopped sharing it after mere hours. One can still find the clip, though, if one knows where to look.

Origin Story: The most popular origin story states that it was filmed in 1971 by Preston Rosewater, IV, a fifth-year senior majoring in film at Midland University. Midland was a small liberal arts university in southern

Tennessee. Rosewater spent a year and over one million dollars to create hundreds of hours of footage. According to legend, Rosewater filmed obscene rituals during on-campus weekend-long drug-fueled orgies. He allegedly learned these rituals from his family. Problems ensued, and most of the million dollars spent went towards paying for damaged people and property. Rosewater's family hired an editor, known only as the Architect, to finish the work when Rosewater proved unable. Legend has it the completed film was shown on the Midland campus at a student gathering in late spring of 1972. The ensuing chaos destroyed Midland and the survivors were institutionalized. Allegedly, the film was confiscated but not destroyed.

Verification: A Midland University existed in south-central Tennessee in 1971, and a young man named Preston Rosewater attended that year. That University was not accredited to grant film degrees and never had a film department. The real Preston Rosewater died in a car accident in 1975 at the age of twenty-five. The real Midland University closed in 1978 and its location is now obscure.

Theater

From: hunter@ntra.org
To: foundation@ntra.org
Re: Report

This is Dwon. Hunter went down to the basement again. I waited at the top until he came back. You know how time goes here, but he was gone for an hour by my count. He was bleeding from the eyes and mouth when he crawled out. I dragged him to the church and put him on a couch. He was still blind when the bleeding stopped so I helped him clean up. We ate and then I tried to get him to talk but he couldn't. When he could see, I got the laptop and he wrote this. You're the only ones who have seen this.

"The air wasn't thick this time. I made it to the theater door with no problems. You have seen the data from that earlier expedition. You know what the Language of Birds is. I'd heard of the concept- I went through a Jethro Tull phase- but encountering something that could grant it is something else. Imagined concept versus incarnate reality. I wanted to be proven wrong: that God exists, that He cares about His creation, and that He will talk directly with His creation.

The theater was shaped like an oval pill, with rounded edges so that the ceiling merged seamlessly into the walls. The projection booth bulged out of one end, and the floor sloped down from there to a projection screen at the other. In between were two rows of six seats facing the screen, split by an aisle down the middle. Fold down crash seats lined the wall.

The twelve theater seats were child sized, luxuriously cushioned, gray leather thrones complete with arm and head rests. The robust five point restraint system (one head, two arms, two legs) incorporated into each one gave me pause. The crash seats folded down from the wall and were
made of hard molded plastic, with no cushioning and no restraints.

I entered the projection booth and tried to start the film. It was a simple automated system, with clearly labeled play, pause, and stop buttons. The power wasn't on. It took a while to find the breaker box in a niche behind the projection equipment. That gave me some time to think about what I was doing.

A ten second clip of this film drove people to hurt themselves, and I was about to watch the whole thing.

But if it was that harmful, then why were they showing it to children? In restraints?

My hands worked on their own while I debated. I remember flipping the power switch. I don't remember pressing the glowing green play button.

On my way out I used a key Dwon gave me to enter an office and collect some documents. I think someone in the criminal justice system will be very interested in them. I know who you are and I know what you're doing. Monsters."

This is Dwon again. Hunter slept after he finished writing and then talked about leaving. I tested his memory by asking questions about his family, and then pretending to forget basic details of our visits to the library and the clinic. He was pretty messed up- he couldn't speak or see sometimes, and other times he'd start bleeding- but he remembered everything. I showed him the sign and packed him into the jeep along with all the material. I'm not sure where he'll come out, but if it's like last time you'll find him and the jeep in northern Illinois. Take good care of him. He's worked very hard for you.

Outside

Dr. Core played the video.

A man sat at a fake wood picnic table. The camera, which was positioned just above and behind the interviewer's right shoulder, zoomed in on his face and then out again. The man wore crisp white scrubs, and his face was clean and pink and his eyes were bloodshot.

Dr. Core consulted her notes. Client completes ADLs on a regular schedule without prompting from staff, she read. "ADLs: Activities of Daily Living," she remembered. "I hate acronyms."

Traces of the interviewer drifted into the shot: the edge of her shoulder, her right hand, wisps of her black hair. "Maria what's her name," Dr. Core thought. "Too bright. Won't last."

Dr. Core paused the video.

The interview was conducted outdoors, which was highly unusual but necessary given the circumstances. The camera angle didn't show it, but Dr. Core knew the table was cemented into a thick slab, and that several HSAs (Human Service Assistants) and one fully-authorized, sedative-equipped RN stood to the side just off camera, ready to assist.

Dr. Core pressed play. The interview began.

Maria: Let's try this again. Please state your name.

Man: [opens his mouth to speak, but only produces a series of hisses, burps, and tweets. Drool leaks from the left corner of his mouth, and he wipes it with a napkin in his right hand.]

Maria: Okay. One more time.

Man: [opens his mouth and forms words with his lips, but the sounds, when they emerge, are again nonsensical. His face flushes red with effort and sweat beads on his forehead. The man bows his head, turns, and spits to the side of the table. A small bird, white with yellow highlights, lands on the back of the man's left hand facing towards him, and chirps brightly. The man sits up straight, looks down at the bird, and smiles.]

Maria: Okay. For the record then, this is Maria Sanchez, second year Therapist Intern, interviewing Hunter Heywood. Mr. Heywood is a white male, forty-one years old, separated but not divorced from his wife of thirteen years. He is father to two children, a son age twelve and a daughter age nine.

He is a former minister of the Episcopal Church.   He has held a series of jobs across the Midwest for the past three years. He was last employed as a private contractor by NTRA. Mr. Heywood came to NewStart from the Rockford Police. He was found wandering the streets, alert and responsive, but unable to speak intelligibly. Medical examinations showed no physical cause.

Mr. Heywood answers questions by writing, although he does lose this ability and totally disconnects from objective reality on an unpredictable and reoccurring basis. Mr. Heywood's responses indicate that he is experiencing substantial memory impairment.

He is not able to remember any events more recent than approximately one year ago, and he has difficulty encoding long and short-term memories in the present. Mr. Heywood is a voluntary client of NewStart Mental Health, and he has been our client for approximately three months. In that time, Mr. Heywood's behavior has been exemplary and he has complied with all treatment opportunities offered to him.

Maria: Is all this accurate Mr. Heywood?

Heywood: [nods. The bird flutters its wings, perches on his left shoulder, and stares into the camera. After a moment it pivots to face Hunter's ear and tweets softly, almost inaudibly. Maria slides a black tablet across the table to Hunter.]

Maria: What does the bird say, Mr. Heywood?

Heywood: [pulls the tablet to him and taps on its surface. A computer-generated voice speaks.] Be at peace. You are loved.

Maria: Staff charted that you remembered something. Could you tell me what that was?

Heywood: [speaking via the tablet] I saw water.

Maria: When did you see water? Where?

Heywood: Under.

Maria: Was the water in something, like a cup?

Heywood: A pool.

Maria: Was anyone in the pool?

Heywood: Children.

Maria: Wh...[begins to speak but is interrupted by loud chirping from the bird on Hunter's shoulder. Still chirping, the bird hops down to Hunter's left hand and then flits out to the table's center, facing Maria. The bird appears to be addressing her.]

Heywood: [opens his mouth and answers the bird in chirps and tweets. The little bird turns to face Hunter while continuing its chirping tirade. Hunter sings in a series of lilting soft notes. The audio abruptly distorts into static while the video blurs into white fuzz.]

[audio and visual resume. Hunter is seated as before, and the bird perches on the crown of his head facing the camera.]

Maria: I. I.

Heywood: [The bird chirps, addressing the camera. Hunter sings. A chorus of bird calls answer from above. The video cuts out.]

Dr. Core stretched in her chair. "Well then," she said to no one. She closed the video and wrote a short email.

From: gloria@newstart.org
To: foundation@ntra.org
Re: Heywood

Heywood situation is stable. Uncertain that anything more will be recovered. Recommend re-housing someplace away from birds, secluded and private, for public safety.

Bill's Arcade Heaven

Adventure

Sherman slung his backpack into the trunk of the rusted Toyota and slammed it shut.

"This is a bad idea," said John. He leaned against the driver's side door. A toothpick twitched left to right between his lips.

"We'll be fine," Sherman said, full of youthful confidence and vigor.

"We're only immortal," quoted John. "For a limited time." He opened the driver's side door and took his position behind the wheel. At seventeen, John Nguyen was five years older than Sherman, which made the situation much more awkward than it already was. "I should drive you home," he said. "This is way too dangerous for anybody, especially us."

"Don't be scared," replied Sherman. "I did research." He turned as he fastened his seatbelt, and the two boys stared at each other.

They thought of their families, and the fact that neither had any other social options. This is all I've got they thought. The shared connection lasted seconds, but spanned emotional light years.

"Right," John said. "Where's the map?"

"Uh," Sherman replied while digging in his pockets. "I've only got the one from Urban, and it's wrong. We've got to pick up the real one from Marek."

"From his house?" John asked, throat constricting around the words, reducing them to an embarrassing squeak.

Sherman understood. "No. He'll meet us in the corner of the Lafargue Elementary parking lot. I paid him yesterday. He's going to pass us the map and that's it. It'll take two seconds."

"Right," John said.

Maps

John parked next to a cluster of tall trees whose leaves were now turning orange and brown.

"They'll fall soon," said John while looking up at the branches. He was thankful they hadn't yet.

"And then snow," Sherman replied.

John cut the engine to conserve gas when five minutes had passed. They rolled the windows down to let a gentle fall breeze stir the air. "I like the fall," Sherman thought. "Not hot, not cold, just right."

"So what's with the maps?" John asked. "You never did explain."

"There are two maps," said Sherman. "One's wrong, and the other's right. Urban has the one that's wrong. His takes you out to some farm in the middle of nowhere.

Last time someone followed it some guy came out and threatened them with a shotgun."

"What?" John asked, voice rising. "Shotgun?"

"You know how farmers are about trespassing," said Sherman. "This guy said they were on his property and he'd shoot if they didn't leave. We're not using that map and we're not going there. Marek has the real map. I paid him twenty dollars. I know he's ripping me off, but I couldn't get it any other way."

"Whoa," John whispered. "Where'd you get twenty dollars?"

"I saved. I was willing to pay double. I'm glad I didn't."

"You don't have it yet."

Sherman nodded. "That's true."

They waited in silence for more than 30 minutes. Wind rustled the leaves without moving the branches. John thought about his sisters. Did they notice he wasn't home? Did they care?

Footsteps crunched on the parking lot gravel, bringing John and Sherman back to the present. Marek rapped on the roof and leaned down to the driver's side window. He wore an olive-green jacket over a black shirt, and his long brown hair hung down into his face for a brief moment, before he pushed it back over his shoulder. "How's it hanging?" he asked playfully.

John stared, and Sherman stammered. "Uh, uh..."

Marek produced an envelope from within the jacket. "Here's what you need," he said, wiggling it back and forth in front of the windshield where they could see, but couldn't reach.

"Right," John said, breaking silence.

"But there's a problem," Marek continued. He put the envelope away and dug in his front pocket. "I can't take your money." He dropped a wad of fives and ones through the window, into John's lap.

Sherman found his voice. "What?"

Marek looked down and to the left as he answered. John could hear him clearly, but Sherman had to strain. "My mom," Marek sighed. "Somebody told." He brought his eyes back up and addressed them directly. "Point is she came down on me, and I was feeling bad anyway.

You're just a kid," he said this to Sherman. "I shouldn't take your money. I'll give you the map anyway, if you tell me the truth."

"What about?" asked Sherman.

"The Meadows," said Marek. "Somebody warned you, right? Bill's Arcade Heaven is real and the games are there. I used to go. But it's weird, man. Serious weird. Not made up."

Sherman leaned in, over the gear shift. "What did you see?"

"I wasn't high," Marek replied. "I didn't do that then. We heard about the games and went to see. I drew the map when we got back. For like a month we were all going. On weekends and after school and we even skipped sometimes." Marek thrust the envelope through the window, barely missing John's nose, and placed it in Sherman's hand.

"I'm giving you the map because I'm not your mama. Go fast and get out." Marek strode away, out of the parking lot towards the apartments on the other side.

Rules

"Pull over there," said Sherman, pointing to a wide spot on the gravel shoulder.

John complied. He shifted into neutral, let out the clutch, and waited.

"There are rules," said Sherman. "Urban says we have to follow them."

John spoke. "Who is Urban? I hear people talk about him but no one says."

Sherman shook his head. "Later. Let me read the rules."

John wasn't pacified. "Why should we care? You said he was wrong."

Sherman shook his head again. "No no," he said, fluttering his hands at shoulder level. "We don't have time to fight. I'll read the rules and then tell you why while we drive. We still have a ways to go."

John scowled but kept silent. Sherman unfolded a paper he produced from his pocket, and began to read.

"Park in the gravel in front of the Meadows boundary posts." Sherman looked up and pointed at the rusted metal posts on either side of the road. "Read these instructions out loud, exactly as I've written them. It is absolutely essential you follow these rules in both letter and spirit. One: take nothing, leave nothing. This includes quarters. All the games are set to free play. If it asks for a quarter something's wrong." Sherman glanced at John and continued. "Two: leave before sunset. Nothing good happens at Bill's Arcade Heaven after dark." John plowed on to the final rule. "Three: children aren't children in the Meadows and especially at BAH. Run if you see children. It's best to leave if you see anyone else at all." Sherman folded the paper and put it in his pocket.

"That's it?" John asked. Sherman shrugged.

John shifted into first and pulled out. "Explain."

Flashback

Sherman knocked and waited. He stood in front of apartment two of the Canterbury Arms Apartments, a run-down, gray- brick apartment complex on the west side of Scofield, IL.

The Canterbury Arms had been decorated to look like a castle in years gone by, complete with circular towers on all four corners and crenellations along the flat roof. Now, the crenellations were black with mold and large cracks gaped where the towers were pulling away from the main building.

Sherman tapped his feet, hoping Dennis Urban would open the door before someone he knew saw and told his parents.

The door opened with a thump and a crack. Sherman stared up at a fat, bald man. Urban's eyes were red and watery, and he wiped his noise with the back of his left hand. An overpowering odor of sweat and spilled beer wafted from within. Sherman considered leaving.

"Sherman?" the man asked. "I'm Dennis Urban, come in." He made no attempt to shake Sherman's hand and did not offer drinks or a place to sit.

Urban kicked clothes and trash out of the way and fell into a recliner in the center of the room. Sherman followed and remained standing a few feet away. The stench was nearly unbearable.

Sherman noticed the worst smells came from a dark hallway to his left. Movement at the edge of vision caught his eye, and he turned to see giant roaches scuttling under a stack of plates in the stained and cluttered kitchenette.

"Here," Urban grunted.

Sherman turned to find the man holding out an envelope.

"This is what you want," he said. "Open it."

Sherman pulled out a packet of maps, illustrations, and densely typed single spaced text.

"That's everything you need." Urban held his hands in a stop gesture. "The maps are wrong, but that's all I've got. You could take that as evidence that something's wrong with the Meadows, or that's something's wrong with me. I don't care."

Sherman endured the stink and remained motionless.

"Nobody's said anything about the interior diagrams of BAH." Urban pronounced the letters separately, as B then A then H. "I don't know if they're accurate. But the games are once in a lifetime. You know arcade games?"

Sherman nodded.

"How old are you?" asked Urban. "You look familiar."

"Twelve," Sherman answered.

"Who's your mother?"

"Stephanie Baxter," Sherman replied.

Urban nodded. "Yep. Went to high school with her. I knew your dad too." Urban pointed over Sherman's shoulder. "Which means you need to go. They won't like you being here. But first, I have to say something."

Sherman waited.

"I was there when it started and everybody thought it was cool. I kept going even after they told us to stop. I know what I'm talking about, even if you think I'm crazy. The games are awesome and worth the trip, but they come at a price. If you follow the rules then the only thing you'll pay is time and gas. If you screw up it can be worse than death."

Urban shifted in his recliner, pointed to the door, and nodded. Sherman ran.

BAH

It was a large rectangle lying on its side in the middle of an open field.

"That's all?" John asked, the first thing he'd said for thirty minutes.

Sherman fidgeted. John had threatened to turn the car around after Sherman told of his visit to Urban. They were so close now- he thought about the mint condition 1989 Ghostbusters upright. He recalled the comprehensive Pac-Man collection. Above all, he remembered his mission. Sherman remained silent.

As they drew closer, they saw that Bill's Arcade Heaven had a gently arched roof and neon blue walls. A square asphalt parking lot in front provided spaces for at least fifty cars. The lot markings were faded and the asphalt was split in many places. "Another winter and it'll be gravel," Sherman thought. A large square sign atop a tall rusted metal pole confirmed that this was indeed, Bill's Arcade Heaven. A wide concrete path led from the lot to the front doors. John parked perpendicular to the path and cut the engine.

"Here we are," he said. "I hope you're right."

Sherman didn't hear; he was already out of the car, waiting for John to open the trunk.

Sherman retrieved his backpack and opened it on the ground. "We need the rest of it," he told John.

"What now?" John asked, his voice flat and hard.

Sherman didn't notice. "We need the packet from Urban." Sherman found the envelope and began to leaf through its contents. "Here it is," he said.

"How to get in," he read. "Pay attention to the sign and the parking lot. If the sign is clean, and the lot is spotless, then the front door will be unlocked. If the sign is dirty, then the front door will be locked and the door on the east side will be open. If it isn't, then the door on the west side should be. If the sign is broken and the lot is cracked, all the doors will be locked but the window will be broken and you can go in that way. Be careful. The window frame is full of glass shards." Sherman looked up but did not look at John.

"Well, the lot's a mess and the sign's ancient," he said. He pointed to a gaping black rectangle in the building's front, just to the left of the front doors. "We go through the window." Sherman rushed to the window and was pulling himself up to the sill before he thought to look back. John stood beside the driver's side door of his Toyota, with one hand on the handle. The skin of his forehead was taught, and his lips were pursed and white.

"What's the problem?" called Sherman.

Flashback

The Scofield Gaming Club met every Thursday at 3pm in study room 3 of the Scofield Public Library. Sherman and John were its only members.

"Why do you hang out with me?" asked John.

Sherman considered the stack of books in front of him: a selection of material from 1980s era Dungeons and Dragons. "You answered the ad," said Sherman.

"I wasn't the only one," John pointed out.

Sherman shuddered, remembering the smell of unwashed bodies in a crowded room. "You were the only one who came back," he said.

"The only one allowed to come back," John corrected.

Sherman's cheeks reddened at the thought. How was he supposed to know so many sketchy old men would show up at a meeting for teenagers? Or that the football team would come just to heckle? He was thankful and at the same time ashamed that library staff had intervened. Future meetings were announced by word of mouth, and specifically restricted to interested teenagers. Mrs. Klock, the head librarian, had made it abundantly clear that another "incident" would permanently end the group.

"Well?' John prompted.

Parking Lot

John and Sherman faced each other. "Well?" John repeated.

"Um," Sherman stalled. "What was the question?"

"Why didn't you tell me everything?"

Sherman shifted from foot to foot. Sweat dripped from his forehead, down his nose, and down into his shirt.

"Race again?" John said.

Sherman stopped fidgeting and his face lightened a few degrees. "No," he said. "Not that. It's..." He lost his voice again.

"Superstition," John finished Sherman's statement. "I told you that's racist and I'm tired of it."

Sherman was close to tears. John lowered his voice and softened his tone. "Look, just tell me what's up. I'm not like my mom."

Sherman shifted one last time and set his backpack on the concrete. "I just wanted to get inside," he whispered.

"We will," John answered in a gentle tone. "I want to know what's there before we go in."

Flashback

"No," said Thomas.

They were talking in Sherman's room, which was the size and shape of a shoe box. Sherman sat on the bed, directly across from his desk and its overflowing bookshelf. Thomas, 18 years old, tall, thin, and shaggy maned, leaned against the door frame with his arms crossed.

"No way," Thomas added.

"But Defender 2!" Sherman objected. "Playable prototype!"

"Still no. I just got the keys back." Thomas glared. "And that place is messed up."

"Granger and them went to the wrong place. That was some farm, and they were trespassing."

"You remember Roach?" asked Thomas. The sudden change of topic caught Sherman off guard, leaving him speechless. "He used to come around here, but he also hung out with Marek. He got the real map and went there back in May."

Sherman shook his head slowly, left to right. This was the first time he was hearing this story.

"He went out by himself and came back three days later." Thomas chuckled. "His mom and stepdad didn't even notice." Thomas drifted into the room and sat next to Sherman. "We noticed, me and Marek and the others. Roach never paid attention to anything. He was always forgetting and nothing got him mad, not even his parents. He'd shrug it all off.

"When he came back he saw everything, especially little kids. He'd get tense when a kid came around, and he'd leave if there was more than one. It didn't look like he was sleeping, either. He kept saying he was there for a few hours in the afternoon and he'd get really mad when we told him he was gone for days. His mom and stepdad sent him away before the start of school. Rumor is that he flipped out on some kid and the judge sent him to a psych ward."

Sherman wrinkled his forehead. "You don't believe rumors," he said.

Thomas chucked again. "Right. But it's true that he went to BAH and that he was gone for three days. I think he got his girlfriend pregnant."

Plan of Attack

John and Sherman shook hands, and then Sherman spread a hand drawn blueprint on the concrete. "We go through that window," he said, and pointed to the gaping hole in the building's facade.

"That puts us in the front lobby." Sherman pointed to the map. "There will be a kitchen to our left where they used to sell snacks and a counter where they sold tickets for admission straight ahead. There's some Pac-Man and DigDug cocktail cabinets there. Urban says they work sometimes, but if you're okay with it I want to pass through the turnstile here," he jabbed the paper, "and go straight into the gaming zone."

"The games are arranged in five sections. Sections one through four have three rows of ten uprights each. That's a total of 120 upright arcade games." Sherman smiled broadly. "Sections one and two are on the ground level. Sections three and four are on a second floor, but they're kinda like wings. There's a big open space in the middle of the second floor that goes from the lobby to the rooms in the back."

"What about section five?" asked John.

"On top of the lobby. That's where they put the pinball machines. Urban says stay out. The whole gaming zone is dimly lit, but section five was pitch black the last time he was here and he got a bad vibe from it."

John sighed. "Uh huh. And what's this?" He pointed to a hallway on the side of the lobby.

"That leads to bathrooms, some office space, and a one way exit that comes out right there." Sherman pointed to a door to their right.

"And what's that?" John pointed to the rooms drawn on the bottom of the map, under the gaming zone.

Sherman hesitated. "Um, Urban doesn't say anything about it. I think it's storage and maintenance. The Defender 2 prototype's in there."

"You're lying," said John.

"No," said Sherman. "I told you everything."

Flashback

"Your mother's worried," she said.

Sherman stood next to the coffee table in the living room. His grandmother sat in a blue armchair to his right. Grandma Baxter was a soft, round woman with curly white hair. Her eyes usually twinkled when she spoke, but today they were flat and dull.

"She thinks you're going out to the BAH," said his grandmother. Sherman stepped back, surprised to hear his plans were so well known.

"Oh, don't worry," Grandma Baxter waved her hand dismissively. "I've got my ears and eyes on everything. Your mother knows because Thomas told her, and he was right to do that." Grandma wagged her finger at him.

"That doesn't matter," she said. "I have a job for you."

Sherman eyed the couch to his left and half sat, half fell into the cushions.

Grandma Baxter ignored Sherman's clumsiness. "You know your grandfather worked for the school board when we moved to Scofield." Sherman didn't know that and he shook his head to show, but his grandmother wasn't looking. She stared up and to his left while continuing to speak. "They were organizing a new district to bring high school students from Mara Plains and Scofield together. Your grandfather was going to serve in administration. They hadn't worked out job titles or responsibilities. They hadn't even decided where this was to happen- if the Scofield kids would go there, if Mara Plains would come here, or if they'd build some new facility in between. But there was lots of money, and your grandfather was positioning himself to reap a substantial harvest."

Grandma Baxter shifted her gaze to Sherman, and he found himself shivering in its bitter cold. "We arrived at the start of June, just a couple days after school ended. Walter, your grandfather Baxter, died thirty days later. We have been provided for, abundantly so." Grandma Baxter paused, and Sherman let out his breath, surprised to find that he'd been holding it.

"Your grandfather left a lot of business unfinished." Grandma pointed a sharp, bony finger and did not ask, but told Sherman, "You," she stabbed the air, "Will finish a part by fetching a book for me."

Sherman knew his grandmother as a gentle, permissive source of comfort and goodness. He didn't know this hard, commanding person and he didn't know how to respond. The best he could muster was a hoarse, incoherent croak.

"Your grandfather had a desk in the back of the BAH, in the corner of the bay where they repaired the machines. They were going to divide up that space and put in offices for administration and counseling services.

'You got to go where the work is,' he liked to say. He did that, and look where it got him." Grandma Baxter's gaze drifted downward and a slight twinkle returned. It took Sherman a moment to realize she was crying.

Eyes still wet, grandma's focus snapped back to Sherman and she stared directly into his eyes. "There was a blue book. It's rectangular, maybe twelve inches wide and six inches tall. You will go to the BAH and bring it here to me." Color began to return to grandma's face. She removed her glasses and wiped the tears from her eyes. Sherman felt tension bleed from his neck and shoulders.

Grandma pulled her purse from the side of the chair where it had been the whole time, and produced a wad of bills. "This will cover any expenses you come across. You keep whatever you don't spend." Grandma smiled. Sherman reached to receive the offering, but grandma didn't let go. "But Sherman?" She asked.

"Yes, grandma?" he replied.

"Whatever you do, don't read the book. Don't even open the cover."

BAH Gaming Zone

Beaming and happy, John reported, "It's all like you said."

Sherman nodded. He heard John's words and responded, but his attention was focused on the double doors at the back of the building. They stood in the center of the gaming zone, between the metal stairs that led up to zones three, four, and five.

"But where's the power come from?" asked John. "Power's off up front, but every machine is on. Not a single one's broken or even dusty. They're all flawless."

"I don't know," Sherman answered tonelessly, eyes blank and face flat.

John paid no attention. "According to the rules, we've got thirty minutes left. I'm going back to Zaxxon and Berzerk."

Sherman stood in place, even as John drifted away towards zone one. "Go ahead," John called, a playful lilt touching his voice. "That's what you came for anyway."

Sherman began walking. "You don't even know," he muttered under his breath.

Flashback

John sat down, hugged himself, and waited.

Dr. Core sat still. Her gray hair was pulled back from her face into a bun. The lenses of her wire rimmed glasses were smudged. John wondered if she noticed.

"So, John," she said, breaking the silence. "How are you this week?"

"Are you really a guidance counselor?" John asked.

"Why do you ask?" she responded.

"Marek says you're not."

"Why do you listen to Marek?"

John scratched the thin hair on his chin. "He grew up here," he said. "He knows."

"Last week we talked about how the others tease and mislead," she said. "This is an example. I am the guidance counselor for Scofield High School. If you wish we can review my credentials together."

"No, thank you," said John, quietly.

"I take it they've been bothering you," Dr. Core said, and leaned forward in her seat.

"Well," John bobbed his head from left to right. "They've been talking, but not like before."

"No more slurs?" Dr. Core prompted.

"No," John confirmed. "But they say."

"What?" asked Dr. Core.

"You make the sick kids worse."

Back Rooms

The double doors swung inward at a light touch. Sherman stepped though into a short hall that ended in a T. Sherman didn't notice the dingy, off-white walls, the popcorn ceiling, or the thin gray industrial carpeting. His attention was focused on the figure sitting in a folding chair next to an end table in the center of the far wall. The figure's shoulder length white hair was green at the tips, and it wore a faded black shirt proclaiming JANE'S ADDICTION, ripped jeans, and dirty blue Converse Chuck Taylors. The figure's hairless smooth skin was the color of milk, and its eyes were raw, red, and watery. Sherman couldn't tell if it was a man or a woman.

"Well?" the figure asked, annoyed and impatient.

Sherman turned to leave.

"Rule three, right?" called the figure as Sherman began walking. "It's too late," it said. "You were screwed the moment you crossed the border. You might as well get what grandma sent you for."

Sherman turned back

"That rule's really about Jose. I haven't seen him today. You best be going."

Sherman hesitated.

"Right or left," the figure said. "You pays your money and you takes your chances."

Sherman chose left.

Acid Police

Sherman opened his eyes. He was lying in a bed on his left side, covered by a thin sheet. His head rested on a comfortable pillow. He sat up and rubbed his eyes, which were crusted as though he'd been sleeping for a long time.

A door opened and a familiar woman entered. She wore her graying hair in a bun, and her thick glasses reflected the overhead light. She sat down in a padded chair at the head of the bed.

"Doctor Core," Sherman said in a raspy voice.

"Yes," she replied.

Sherman rubbed his eyes again. "What," he said, "Are you doing here?"

Dr. Core raised an eyebrow. "I'm checking on you," she answered. "What," she paused, mimicking his delivery, "Are you doing here?" She smiled, and Sherman scooted back on the mattress until he pushed against the cold concrete wall. "What do you remember?"

"I," Sherman scratched his head. "I remember..." he drawled, and then he told Dr. Core of the trip out to Bill's Arcade Heaven. He told of the maps, the rules, and of his conversations with John. He told of the arrival, of their entrance, and about the video games they played.

"The back room, Sherman," Dr. Core prompted. "What about the back room?"

"Assed Poleeshay," Sherman sung to an odd tune.

Dr. Core waited. Her face showed no emotion: not alarm, not surprise, and not anger or sadness.

Sherman continued to sing the odd phrase in a continuous loop: "Assed Poleeshay! Assed Poleeshay!" His eyes glazed and his nose began to bleed.

Dr. Core produced a tissue. "Clean yourself," she commanded, interrupting.

Sherman blinked and took the tissue, but he didn't know what to do with it until Dr. Core showed him.

"You're bleeding," she said. "There."

Sherman complied.

"What was that?" she asked. "Where did you go?"

"I can't..." Sherman mumbled. "It's still there."

"You can't say without going," Dr. Core intuited.

"There are drugs for that."

***

Later, how much Sherman could not say, Dr. Core handed him a little white cup containing multicolored tablets and a glass of water.

The world stopped rushing. He hadn't noticed until it stopped. A door closed on the room filled with singing. He could breathe without fear. Sherman felt very sleepy and he began to slide sideways.

"Not yet," said Dr. Core. "We need to talk first."

Sherman nodded. "Okay," he whispered.

"Good," said Dr. Core. "Now tell me what you saw."

***

ACID POLICE was sprayed in big red letters on the hallway wall. What did it mean? There was a rhythmic thumping coming from further down, or was it coming from under his feet? And there was singing...

Sherman's vision cracked into a million shards of white, red, and black. Fire spread along his right cheek and dribbled from his eyes. Dr. Core stood above, left hand raised to deliver another slap.

"I am sorry," she said in a flat tone, "But I can't let

you go." She lowered her hand and scratched her chin. "There is another way. Sleep. I will return."

Interview

The police officer wasn't dressed properly. That was John Nguyen's first impression. The man wore a white polo shirt and khakis, with his badge clipped to his belt on his right hip. John thought he should be wearing his uniform: a blue or brown button-down shirt with badges and insignia, paired with dark pants and an equipment belt. John shifted in his chair and tried to focus. How could he trust him, if the officer couldn't be counted on to dress right when it mattered?

"We shouldn't talk until your parents get here," said the officer. His name was James Park, and he'd asked John to call him "Jim." John addressed him as "officer" and "sir."

"They're not coming, sir," said John.

Officer Park scratched his head. "Well, I've got permission," he said. "But I don't like it. Your mom and dad should be here." He paused, and getting no response from John, continued. "So let's start there. Why aren't your parents coming?"

"Dad's working and mom's sick."

The officer smiled. "Where does your dad work?"

"He does import- export," John explained. "He travels a lot overseas. I think he's in China right now."

"You think?" the officer prompted.

"Yes," John answered. "On my sixteenth birthday he told me that I'm a man and that I would run the house when he's away."

"Okay," said the officer.

"I have six older sisters," said John. "When dad left, Rie and Jun said I would never tell them what to do."

The officer nodded.

"And that was that. Dad travels for at least six months at a time. Rie and Jun run the store and handle the stateside business. I go to school and stay out of the way."

"Where's your mother?" asked the officer.

"Sick," quipped John.

"I'm sorry," said the officer. "It's long term, I take it? Is it serious?"

John shook his head, embarrassed. "Mental," he replied. "Not physical."

The officer waited until John continued.

"She's my dad's second wife. The first died in labor

about 20 years ago, having my sixth older sister. They came to the US from Vietnam in the seventies. Dad fought in the war with the ARVN. He's seventy-five, and my mom's forty. My dad says he remarried because he wanted a son."

The officer continued smiling and nodding.

"My mom was born and raised in Chicago. She'd never lived outside of the city until we moved here, and she's never been out of Illinois."

"But," prompted the officer.

"Yes," said John. "She says she's a priestess from Huė, and that she's over a hundred years old. She's always talking about signs and symbols, and good and bad spirits. Dad doesn't care, he's atheist. My sisters are Catholic."

"Which leaves you?" asked Officer Park.

"Nowhere," answered John. "Absolutely nowhere. Mom won't leave the house because she might get possessed. Rei and Jun won't let me anywhere near the business. They feed me, give me money for clothes and gas, and tell me to get lost. So I do."

"You went to Bill's Arcade Heaven with Sherman Tyndale."

John sighed. "Yes."

"How'd you come to be his friend, anyway?"

John sighed again. "He talked to me."

"There was no one else?" asked the officer.

"You mean no one else like me?" snapped John. "No other Vietnamese?"

The officer shrugged.

John slouched low in his chair. "I'm too Western," he whispered. "And too secular. I don't go to mass. I don't speak Vietnamese."

Officer Park sat forward in his chair. "Wow," he commented. "But what about the other kids in your grade?"

"Do you live here, officer?" John snapped. "I don't exist to them."

Officer Park rubbed his chin. "Hmm. Well, back to the BAH. What happened after Sherman went into the back?"

Searching

Stephanie bruised her knuckles on the door, producing a sharp metallic echo from beyond. She stood back and watched the clock on her phone. Thirty seconds passed, and then a minute. She stepped forward to knock again, but a buzzer sounded and the door clicked open.

Inside, Stephanie followed a smooth gray hall tiled in white squares to a place where three halls intersected in a Y. The hall she'd followed formed the base, and before her, between the two branching halls that formed the arms, there was a waist high counter in front of a small room. Stephanie could see a computer screen and a panel with a big red button on the far wall, but most importantly, a thick man with buzz cut gray hair stared at her impassively from a rolling chair.

"Yes?" he asked.

"I'm here for my son," she answered.

"No one's here," he said.

"Well," she was flustered. Heat rose in her cheeks and she fought tears. "You know where he is."

The man, still seated, continued to glare. "I don't," he said. After a moment he added, "You should leave."

"You let me in!" she objected.

"No," the man asked, lowering his voice. "I didn't. I don't know who did."

Soft footsteps to her right announced a new arrival. Stephanie saw another man, this one thinner than the first, wearing blue scrubs and a white lab coat.

"Ms. Baxter," he said. "Who told you to come here?"

"Tyndale," she spat. "My name is Tyndale."

"Here for her son," the seated man droned. "I didn't buzz her in."

"Of course not," the coated man answered. "It's time to go," he said to Stephanie.

"But Sherman!" she objected.

"No," said the coated man. "You know you have to leave. I'm sure you'll be contacted later."

The man in the lab coat held Stephanie's right arm just above the elbow and turned her around.

Together, they walked back the way they came.

Pictures

The room was hot and crowded. Electronic components crammed onto rolling carts and bolted into niches on tall shelves hummed and blinked. Hastily mounted screens displayed graphs and scrolling lists of code. Wires snaked along the walls, floor and ceiling, and converged on one of a dozen connections on Sherman's prone body.

"Okay," a voice called over an intercom. "Fire it up."

The components harmonized. A five foot by three-foot screen on the wall lit up, first pure blue, and then...

A poorly lit room. A flashlight roamed its interior and lingered on a sign that read

SPACE FLIGHT
BASE ASSAULT

The light shined on a chair in front of a wall sized plate glass window. The glass was very dirty. Nothing could be seen beyond when the light shone directly on it. Indirect, angled attempts provided slight glimpses of a shadowed globe and lumps on the floor.

The light swung back to the dust covered chair, which looked like a cross between a leather recliner and a hydraulic seat you'd find at a dentist's. A joystick was placed below the crotch, between the two legs.

Disembodied hands set the flashlight on the floor. The view shifted as the unseen body settled into the chair and hands gripped the control stick. A rainbow of colorful light cascaded, and then then there were stars, streaming past a cockpit. The cockpit view shifted to the left, and a large globe filled the screen. Details emerged as the globe approached: deep channels formed a maze across its surface. Tall, spiky towers were spaced evenly along the channel walls, but all were silent and dark.

Perspective shifted again, and the ship raced downward, into the deepest, longest channel. Towers raced by, and the ship drew down low, into the very center and increased speed. An alarm sounded. Lights flashed. A hand reached up and slapped them off. Everything rushed and blurred. The channel ended dead ahead, yet the ship did not pull up. A great tower, the largest of them all, loomed above. The ship dipped, launched a missile, and pulled up at the last possible moment. There was a great white light, the sound of debris pelting metal and...

The chair lay on its side. Light glinted off of a million shards of glass. Flames poured from a globe on a pedestal. Smoke filled the room. The view blurred, shuddered, and went dark.

"Well shit," a voice said over an intercom.

Interview

"The room blinked," said John. "And then it was different."

Officer Park scratched his head. "What does that mean?"

John shrugged, and then began to explain. "When you blink everything goes black for a second. Most people don't notice because it happens so fast. Sometimes, a blink takes longer, like if your eyes itch because you're sleepy. But whatever, everything goes black."

Officer Park's cheeks colored a light pink, and he sighed loudly. "Right," he said, while clenching and releasing his right hand in a stress release exercise his therapist showed him a week earlier.

"This was like the room blinked. My eyes were open and the lights were on, but everything went black. Not dark. Black, like nothing was there. And it lasted more than a second, like a long blink when you rub your eyes."

"And then?" Officer Park drew circles in the air with his finger, trying to move the conversation along.

"The whole place was older. Before, the uprights were all on, and there were lights on overhead. Now the power was out. Not a single cabinet was on. Some had broken screens, and a few were lying on their sides. Light came in through big holes in the roof. There were piles of metal and insulation, and electric wires were all over the place. I looked over at a cabinet I just played, and it wasn't the same. I mean- I played a mint upright cabinet of Super Pacman, and now it was burned out shell with a caved in screen and Korean writing on the side along with a few peeling Pacman stickers. It was a trashed counterfeit."

Officer Park cocked his head to the right and stopped flexing his hand. "And then?"

"I got scared and went to find Sherman. The double doors that had been there before were lying on the ground. I walked down a short hall and took a right."

Officer Park scooted forward in his seat. "Okay. What next?"

"There was all kinds of junk on the floor, and it was dark. Sherman had the flashlight, but my phone was in my pocket so I used the flashlight app."

The officer nodded as he took notes.

"Just after I turned right I found a clear trail of footprints. The floor was wet and mucky, with mold and other stuff. It stunk, but not enough to make me sick."

"Or to make you turn around," suggested the officer.

"Yes," said John. "I followed the footprints down the halls and through holes in the wall. I kept going over piles of trash, balancing on beams, and trying to stay out of big puddles."

"The footprints kept going?" asked the officer.

"Yes," said John. "They were always clear, and they never doubled back. I don't know how long I was back there, but it seemed like hours. And the hallways were super long and dark. It didn't feel like I was in the same building. Sherman showed me a diagram before we went in and the back room wasn't that big. It should have took me ten, maybe twenty minutes, to search the whole thing. But the footprints kept going and I followed."

"And then?" prompted the officer.

"There was an open place. I smelled it before I got there. It stunk so bad, it made me want to throw up. Like if you mixed up mold, trash, and poop in a bowl and heated it in a microwave."

Officer Park scowled. "Sounds awful."

"I want to puke thinking about it. And the room was worse." John took a deep breath and shook his head from side to side. "The whole roof had collapsed and crushed whatever was under it. There were all these long, thick metal beams from the roof, sticking out from piles of mush. I could see these bits of black mixed in with everything else; maybe that was the shingles or something. All the way across I could see the open shell of the other side of the building. But in between, everything was covered with birds and bird poop." Officer Park leaned in and paid close attention. They'd asked him to document any mention of birds.

"Birds were everywhere," John continued. "And the poop was deep, like inches or maybe even feet. I wasn't going in there."

"But the footprints?"

"Went right in. They sunk in deep, and led up and over to an upright cabinet in the corner."

"You could see this from where you stood?"

"Yes sir," John replied. "I couldn't see all the footprints, but I could see enough."

"What about the birds?" asked the officer.

"Every one of them was watching me. Not one flew away."

"Did they make sounds? Squawk?"

"No sir," said John. "Not a sound. It was super quiet. Then the cabinet turned on."

"Okay."

"It was loud, but they still didn't fly. It was on attract mode, where the game plays itself to show what it's like. It would play a few seconds of music and then there would be the game sounds, and then it would repeat."

"And the birds stayed still?"

"Yes. But I wasn't going into that mess. The footprints closest to me went down deep into that muck. I didn't see Sherman."

"So you left?"

"I turned to go and saw somebody out of the corner of my eye. I turned back to look and he was still there, standing way up top on a fallen cross beam. He was a short kid with black hair and brown skin. It was so bright I couldn't see more."

Officer Park wiped sweat from his forehead. He had to be very careful now. They would want to know all of this, down to the smallest detail. "So," he began. "Exactly what did you see?"

"I already told you," said John before continuing. "The kid called out to me. He said, 'I know you're looking for Sherman. He is not here.' The smell got bad. Maybe a breeze pushed a cloud in front of the sun, because the light got dim. I got dizzy and started to puke.

All I could think was to stay out of the bird shit. I didn't even care about puking on myself. I was bending over and it felt like I was going through spirals, around and down. The puke kept coming and I kept getting lower. I saw there were all kinds of little bones in the white shit."

"Birds," stated Officer Park.

"Some," said John. "Not all. I saw a little hand just as I was going in face first with my mouth open."

"A doll," the officer suggested.

"Dolls don't have bones," said John. "But it all rushed away. I was looking at the short kid's shoes. They were worn out Keds. There was no bird shit on them. I heard him say, 'You're going to have to get Sherman yourself.' This heavy thing fell in my lap. 'Bring that,' he said. 'That's what you came for.'"

Officer Park's upper thighs bumped the table painfully as he tried to stand. "Calm down," he thought. "Don't bungle it now." He settled back into his seat. Sweat coated his body and streamed down his forehead. "So..." he asked, struggling to sound casual. 'What was it?"

"A book," John said. "A big black rectangle book. Inside there was all this weird writing around pictures of bodies on a blue background. The bodies were all taken apart. It looked like an assembly manual that comes with a Lego kit."

Color drained from the officer's face. "You looked at it? How much?"

John ignored the questions. "It wasn't thick but it was heavy. It was really hard to carry. I think I was really sick."

"Where is it?" asked Officer Park, gaining control for a moment.

"I gave it to the lady."

"Lady?" asked the officer.

"The one that met us at the border. You know."

"No, I don't," said the officer.

"She said she was Sherman's grandmother." John frowned. "Don't you want to hear how I found Sherman?"

Reunion

Mother and son hugged each other tightly in the corner of the consultation room. Three white coated men huddled next to the door. Stephanie ignored their conversation, even though it was clearly audible from where she sat. "I have my son," she thought to herself.

"That's all that matters."

One of them, short and wide with brown skin, waddled over and cleared his throat.

Stephanie fixed him with a hostile glare. "What?"

"There are some questions..." he began. Stephanie glared until he stopped mid-sentence.

"We want to leave," she stated. "We're not talking."

Another white coat drifted over. This one was tall and wore blue scrubs under his coat. "You can't," said the tall one. "You stay until we say."

"Then say," quipped Stephanie. "You've done enough. Taken enough."

"Hardly," replied the tall one. "Your family has lived well, and now it's time to pay the piper."

Stephanie gasped and tightened her grip on Sherman, who began to wriggle under the pressure but did not complain.

"Gentlemen," said the third. He held his hands up in a placating gesture, and smiled broadly. The frames of his metal glasses matched the color of his thinning gray hair.

"We can solve this with one question," he said to Stephanie. "Just one, and you're on your way."

Stephanie glared, and the man in the glasses

continued. "Where's your mother? We need to find her."

Stephanie laughed. "That's it? I only know what she tells me, and you," she fixed each with a harsh, smoldering stare, "know she lies."

"Right, well," the short one said, "Her habits. Where would you start looking?"

"Up your own ass," she said.

Blue Book

Olivia Baxter put the book on the table. "Are you happy now?" she asked.

Dr. Gloria Core grimaced. "A high price," she replied. "It had to be paid."

"My daughter will never trust me," whispered Olivia. "And Sherman."

"Will be looked after and always receive the best in care," said Dr. Core. She picked up the book. "This will go with the other three. Now there's only one remaining."

Olivia shook her head. "Of the blue series. Then there's the green and the gray..."

"Ssss," hissed Dr. Core. "Some things!" she touched her hand to her mouth. They stared at the empty table in silence. "We can't stop," she said, finally. "Or have you lost the desire to give birth to a dancing star?

Olivia sighed, and gave the proper response. "No," she said. "I still have chaos in me."

Brown Lake

Better Man

V: Art thou satisfied?

R: No. I adore greatness and I long for distant shores.

V: Dost thou despise thyself?

R: Yes. I despise myself and all present happiness, reason, and virtue.

V: What dost thou desire?

R: I desire frenzy. I desire lightning.

V: Dost thou have chaos in thee?

R: Yes, and I strive to give birth to a dancing star.

(excerpted from the Liturgy of the Better Man, also known as the Red Rite)

A Visit With Friends

"What do you want to tell me?" Charles asked the white coat. They were sitting in rocking chairs on the back porch of the infirmary. The overgrown field sloped downward beneath them, ending at the muddy banks of the brown lake from which the camp drew its name.

The technician in the white coat adjusted his black rimmed glasses. "Um, I don't know," he replied.

"You do," Charles insisted. "You always do."

"Always?" the white coat muttered. "But I," he said and stopped.

"No," Charles said after a moment of silence. "No buts. No judgment. Say what you must."

"Well," the white coat began. "I'm sorry. I didn't know."

"What didn't you know?" asked Charles.

"What they were doing," said the white coat. "They didn't tell us. They put us in a room and showed us the code. We didn't know what it was for or what it did."

Charles nodded. "And now?"

"I'm sorry. I never meant to hurt anyone."

Charles nodded again. "You can rest," he said. "It wasn't you and it's not your fault. What's done is done."

"Will you," the white coat whispered. "Can you?"

"Forgive?" asked Charles. "Yes."

"But," prompted the white coat.

"Yes," Charles answered. "I speak only for me. I can't say about the others."

"But what about him?" asked the white coat, in a louder voice.

"Jose?" asked Charles. "I don't talk to him anymore."

A Three Hour Tour

Urbex offers tours of abandoned industrial, medical, and military sites.
Safe and 100% legal.
Photographers especially welcome.
No ghost hunters, please.
Contact us at

They met in the game room at Tom's Bar and Grill, which was located in a stretch of woods a few miles north of the Wisconsin-Illinois border. Jillian assumed it was a part of some town or village, but she saw no point in finding out. It was here and so was she. Now was the time to get down to business. Four others were present: the tour leaders, Leonard and Lisa; and the couple, Aiden and Bri; for a total of five.

"So," said Leonard, and he clapped his hands, softly. He was a thin man, and wore his steel gray hair in a long ponytail. Jill eyed his faded Grateful Dead tie-dye shirt, hemp necklace complete with crystal, and wire rimmed glasses, and wondered if he could be more stereotypical. "Lisa and I are your guides for the trip to Brown Lake." He motioned to the woman next to him, who gave a little bow.

Lisa, on the other hand, kept her black hair from her eyes with a backwards facing baseball cap, and wore a long sleeve Carhartt shirt with muddy jeans and leather boots. Lisa said, "I'm the one that answers your texts and emails. We've got some legal stuff to go over, but before that, does anyone have questions?"

"Yeah, actually," said Bri. She was a young woman with blond hair, and wore a University of Wisconsin sweatshirt over yoga pants. She pointed at Leonard and asked "Are you the owner?"

"No," said Lisa. "The owner, Jerry Lawson, doesn't lead tours anymore."

"Um," Bri said, shifting from one foot to the other while staring at her feet, "My dad, I mean, I, specifically asked for a tour with the owner."

Leonard remained silent. "Yeah," Lisa answered. "And Jerry told Mr. Lytle, your father, that wasn't possible. And then he called me and Leo, because we're his best team."

"Oh," said Bri, leaning into a side hug from her boyfriend, a broad shouldered, flannel wearing, bearded young man named Aiden.

Lisa and Leonard directed the three to a nearby table, where they sat while Lisa explained legal limitations and presented them with documents for signing. When that was done, Lisa nodded to Leonard, who produced a map from a large cloth bag that had been lying against the wall.

"This is Brown Lake," he said, unfurling the map. Leonard jabbed his right index finger at a blue blob. "It's brown in real life. We'll park here," he pointed above the blob, "and walk around the camp to here." He jabbed a spot to the side. "This map does not show the camp. In fact, there are no maps of the camp, but that's not unusual."

Leonard continued, "Jerry says the camp's north of the lake. There are a bunch of smaller buildings down by the water that were probably cabins for campers, and three or four big buildings at the top of the hill that were used for activities."

"I thought he didn't do tours," said Bri.

"He doesn't," replied Leonard. "Jerry does research and sets up the tours. He got a tip from a reliable friend about this place. He's never been there, and neither have I."

"Which brings us to safety," said Lisa. "We usually scout a property before bringing a tour. This is a special exception."

"The bus," said Jill.

"Yep," said Lisa. "The infamous Stabbin Cabin. Does everyone know the story?"

Bri and Aiden shook their heads.

Lisa asked Jill, "Do you want to tell it?"

"It's an urban legend based on a real story," Jill began. "The legend is that a fraternity got kicked off the campus of a university for misbehavior, and that instead of giving up, they bought a school bus and turned it into a mobile party station. The fraternity, bus and all, disappeared during a night of wild partying."

"What about the name?" asked Bri.

Jill sighed and shook her head. "Think about it."

Aiden whispered into Bri's ear and her eyes widened. "But now they found the bus," said Jill.

"Yep," agreed Lisa. "The tipster sent photos to Jerry that might be that bus. It's got the name painted on the side, and it's in the right condition for thirty years."

"But why would it be there?" asked Bri. "And what's the real story?"

Jill shook her head and Lisa intervened. "You can look it up online. To get back to safety, the point is that there's greater risk involved in this trip than usual. The tipster reported seeing dogs roaming in packs, and he said they seemed aggressive. I'm going to bring a gun. If you have a problem with that, you can back out now and get a full refund."

Jill and the couple remained silent.

"That's settled," said Lisa. "You may not bring your own gun. I have years of hunting experience and I am an Army veteran. I do not want you shooting me on accident."

Again, silence prevailed.

"Good. See you all bright and early in this parking lot at seven A.M. on Saturday."

The Stabbin Cabin

(excerpted from an online article)

April 1987. A bus transporting 23 people disappeared over the weekend. The bus was owned and operated by the Alpha Brotherhood, a local social fraternity. Area police had eye witness reports of drinking and drug usage on the bus throughout the evening, up to the time of its disappearance. Police stopped the bus at 8pm, but found no grounds to detain the driver or the passengers. When questioned by a journalist for the Milwaukee Journal, Deputy Bradley Hoyt said, "They didn't break any laws and everyone was sober. Yes, that name was painted on the bus, but as I understand it, that's not illegal even if it is offensive."

The Alpha Brotherhood was a local fraternity on the campus of the Southern Wisconsin Agricultural College until late January of 1987. At the beginning of January, three members of the fraternity were charged with sexual assault and lewd behavior over conduct at a party in their fraternity house. The charges were dismissed two months later in March, but prior to that College administrators revoked the Alphas right to meet on campus. Alumni of the Alpha Brotherhood initiated a lawsuit against the College in late March, following the dismissal of the charges. Current members of the Brotherhood organized a protest of their own, concurrent with the lawsuit. The Alphas contended that their freedom of speech and right to assembly were being unjustly curtailed. To protest, they bought a retired school bus and publicly declared in a full page ad in the Journal that, "We do not accept the ruling of the Southern Wisconsin Agricultural College's administration, and we intend to continue regular meetings of the Alpha Brotherhood on the publicly owned streets of Dodgeville, Wisconsin in our privately owned and fully insured bus, which will henceforth be known as The Stabbin Cabin. Sic semper tyrannis!"

A Visit With Friends

A young man was pacing the back porch when Charles arrived. The man wore a red polo shirt with pressed khaki pants, but his curly black hair was an uncombed, lopsided tangle.

"Ancient Greek religion was more honest," the young man declared as Charles sat. "The educated class understood the pantheon to be allegorical and not literal. Thus, the gods were representations of mankind's innate capabilities. They knew that they were powerful and that they could be gods. They didn't offer worship or subservience. Rather, they acknowledged what was and what could be." The young man stopped to take a breath.

"Who are you?" asked Charles.

The young man ignored Charles and continued.

"This Christianity, with its sacrifice, pseudo-morals, and good guy badges undid all that was good in Greek and Roman philosophy. The Christian god not only tolerated weakness and imperfection, it promoted doing so! It blessed the weak and the poor, and propped up those who could not stand on their own. Just look at its so-called savior, a divine man who allegedly has power over everything and yet allows himself to be snuffed out by his inferiors! This so-called redeemer doesn't even help his followers- he shows he can do so by curing some, but then refuses to do so for all! If one has power, one is obligated to use it!" The young man's face was glowing red, and sweat dripped freely from the sharp edges of his jaw. He leaned on the arm of a nearby chair and gasped for air.

"Can I help you?" asked Charles, in a low voice.

"One must not settle," the young man began again. "One must strive. One must reach. One must become. To do otherwise is to betray one's manhood and return to the lesser, animal state. Our calling is to become a bridge between this lowly present and the exalted future. We must not settle."

"Is this how you usually talk to friends?" interrupted Charles.

The young man's eyes, which had been focused on something far away, now zeroed in on Charles.

"Friends?" asked the young man. "Does an eagle befriend a worm? Can a grain of sand befriend the ocean? Know your place."

"I think I know who you are," said Charles.

Expedition

The five members of the Urbex tour to Brown Lake marched single file downhill, across the camp property. To their right was the muddy, oil slicked, kidney shaped lake. To their left, three large buildings stood at the top of the hill. Directly ahead, stood a row of cabins.

Lisa, wearing a brown canvas jacket and carrying a pump action twelve-gauge shotgun, walked at the front. Leonard, unarmed but conspicuously alert, watched the rear. Bri, Aiden, and Jill slogged along at a steady pace in the middle.

"We pass the cabins on the right and go halfway around the lake, "Lisa announced over her shoulder. "Then we follow an access road through the forest and we're there."

Jill grunted. The grass was short, but the ground was uneven and surprisingly soft. She worried about twisting an ankle. "How are they going to get me out, if I can't walk?" she wondered. "There's no way an ambulance is coming to the Meadows."

Ahead, Bri and Aiden seemed unconcerned. Aiden wore boots and jeans with a waterproof jacket, and carried an expensive camera on a strap around his neck. Bri wore furry brown boots, a bright pink jacket, and yoga pants. At the start of the trek she'd complained about getting dirty, and Aiden had done the group a favor by gently shushing her.

The group approached the cabin closest to the lake. A wooden number six was nailed to the siding above the cabin's front door.

"Old Army barracks," a voice called from the other side.

A man stepped out from the shadows. He carried a rifle, which was pointing at the ground. Lisa's shotgun twitched in her hands.

"Whoa now," the man said, and he bent to set the rifle down. "We're all friends here." Lisa turned her gun around slowly, and rested it butt-first next to her right foot.

"Okay," the man said, "Better. My name is Richard." He was a lean man with a weathered face and short gray hair. He wore an old denim shirt and stained brown pants with the cuffs rolled up.

"What are you doing here?" asked Lisa.

"I live here," said Richard. "Yourself?"

"We're leading these three," Lisa gestured, "to the car lot on the east side."

"I heard you say you'll go by the lake," said Richard.

"Yes."

"I highly recommend you go up the hill to the road and follow the edge of the forest to get there. It's safer."

"Then we can drive!" quipped Bri.

Richard shook his head. "You could, but it won't help. There's some pretty deep ditches and a bunch of soggy spots where you'll get stuck. You might as well walk."

"Through the forest is faster," said Lisa. "And we're on a schedule."

"Okay," said Richard. "There are dogs in there. And that access road doesn't always go all the way through."

Lisa nodded. "I know," she said. "I've come prepared." She hefted the shotgun.

Richard stared. "I'm coming with," he said, finally.

Pools of Consciousness

"The commercial internet was new. The principle of connectivity that it represented excited us. We looked at the current tech and thought ahead to the future, when humans would move past networking of devices to networking of minds. Then we discovered the military already had this ability and had chosen not to develop it.

"If there is a god, then it would be the sum total of human consciousness. In seeking to network humans, we sought to incarnate a god. Not a god of myth and legend. A real, corporeal presence that transcends our current limitations. But a truly transcendent higher power cannot end in humanity; it must go beyond. Networking fully socialized human adults wouldn't get us there; it would produce super powered humans akin to the Greek and Roman gods. We needed to network unformed, presocialized humans. The more malleable and the less shaped the better.

"We wanted the true essence of the minds to meet, mix, and meld. Without the constructed layers added by experience: we desired the true essence, the raw is-ness at the core of the person. Sensory data was to be eschewed. Thus, the plan was to network the ideal subjects in a pool of blood-warm saline-rich water, which would be housed in a totally dark and soundless room. We'd connect them in sensory deprivation tank, if you will.

"Once we achieved the initial gestalt, we would expand the boundaries, starting with all other branches of hominoidea. Then we'd move on to canines, felines, and really, anything with a central nervous system that could tolerate the networking process. The more perspectives the better. But keep in mind, this would only happen after the gestalt formed. The higher would rule the lower, as befits our nature. And finally, the coup de grace, we would bring the expanded, yet still organic gestalt, to the inorganic. We would connect it to digital intelligence, and thereby allow it to expand worldwide. The internet would become its nervous system! And we, we would be those who truly became bridges! Those who reached beyond, to give birth to a dancing star!

"But... everything went wrong. We stumbled, and the Last Man prevailed.

A Visit with Friends

The red shirt was worn out. He sat in a chair on the porch, red faced and panting for breath.

"It started with a dream," he said after a minute. He continued at a slower pace and in a calmer tone of voice. "There was a large group of children standing in a basin. There were more than a hundred. The vision expanded and blurred, and the children were joined by their grandparents, in wheelchairs, with walkers, and even lying on the ground. There were four grandparents for each child, so now there were more than four hundred in the basin. It was so crowded. They struggled for space, and mewled for rescue, but without passion. Then the wind blew and the vision blurred. There was a motion, and a light and the sound of a bell ringing. The young and the old melted." He paused to take a breath.

"Yes, they melted," he confirmed, even though Charles remained silent. "They melted and mixed into an orange stew. Its surface was slick and smooth, like plastic. The wind moved upon it but it did not stir. The vision receded and I saw that the basin was full, to the very brim. But then, there was movement and a light and a bell. Wind from within stirred and frothed the mix. Heat and light burst forth." The red shirt gulped and took a deep breath. Charles considered fetching a glass of water but decided against it.

"Then there was another movement, and a bell with no light. The plastic mix boiled, burned, and steamed. It became a cloud. They, the young and the old, became clouds, soaring high above. They spread and contracted as they mixed. And they chose the currents. They made them, and rode them where they willed." The man in the red shirt hung his head low so that his chin touched his chest.

"Is that it?" Charles asked. "Is that what you came to say?"

The red shirt roused. "He who has ears, let him hear."

Expedition

Richard walked near the back of the group with Jill. He carried his rifle in the crook of his right arm, with the muzzle pointing down and away.

"They brought the cabins over from a decommissioned Army base," he said to no one in particular. "They were WWII barracks. I think they got them for free, if they'd pay for transport. I bet they had connections and got free labor. Things were different then."

"Who's they?" asked Jill. "When was this?" They walked down the access road at a brisk pace. The sun was shining and the light breeze did little to dispel the rising heat. Jill considered removing her fleece jacket.

"A church group," Richard answered. "Methodists built the camp, I think. One member gave the land, another located the barracks, and another arranged their transport. All for no or minimal cost. The whole thing was done ultra-cheap. They built a cafeteria, lounge, chapel, and infirmary on site, using the finest cinderblocks and white paint available. They did spend a little to put stained glass in the chapel- but they did that abstract fragmented glass stuff that was so popular in the sixties."

"The sixties?" asked Jill. The rest of the group ignored the conversation. Only Leonard remained in the back with Jill, and he made a point of looking anywhere but at Richard.

"Yep," answered Richard. "The early 60s, at the latest. That's the best I could do."

"With what?"

"Records we found," he said. "In the basement of the infirmary, where we live."

The twin ruts in the road disappeared into tall grass and brush. Trees leaned into the open space. The group formed into a line and marched single file. Everyone but Richard held their breath, waiting to see if something waited to spring from the thick woods on either side. "The beast in the jungle," Jill thought. Even Richard, who had to this point been lecturing about the deficiencies in the camp construction, now lapsed into silence and gripped his rifle with both hands. The sunlight from above flickered and grayed as clouds massed. The branches were thick and cast shadows on the ground below. Jill heard no birdsong and saw no movement from anything- not even a pesky gnat.

The group pressed on. The shadows thickened and darkened, to the point that Jill began to wonder if the sun was setting. Then they were out. Bright white light blinded Jill, her toe caught, and she stumbled sideways into an unyielding smooth object. Jill blinked. It was the hood of a car. A rusty white Honda, to be exact. She looked left and right and a row of cars, trucks, and vans parked side by side stretched away in either direction as far as she could see. Behind the Honda she could see an open space the width of two cars and then another row of cars parked nose to nose.

"Ladies and gentlemen, the graveyard," announced Richard. The rest of the group was already past this first row. Jill could see Aiden stalking down the aisle to her right, camera raised, snapping away. Lisa and Leonard stood together to her left. Leonard appeared calm and unconcerned, but Lisa frowned and held her shotgun close.

Jill skirted around the Honda and approached. "Where's Bri?" she asked.

"That way," Leonard replied, motioning up and over the opposite row. Lisa paid no attention. Jill squeezed past an orange VW Bug, a Ford Maverick, and a couple of 80s subcompacts and came out into another open aisle. Richard followed. Bri stood in the middle, facing away. She carried her coat over her right arm. "Jill," she called. "Is that the bus you're looking for?"

The bus, which was clearly labeled THE STABBIN CABIN in bold black letters on the side, was parked lengthwise along the aisle, with the passenger side facing out. The folding door at the front was pulled shut. Thick shrubs and bushes grew from underneath, and a small tree was coming up on the back by the emergency exit. Jill noticed the tires were still inflated.

"Weird," she told Bri. "They were flat in the photos. And there were barely any bushes. And..."

"You got to see photos?" Bri whined. "They wouldn't show us anything. It was like they didn't want us to come."

Jill shrugged and stepped up to the folding door. Gentle pushes proved it would flex. "Not rusted shut," she muttered. Harder pushes failed to bend them open.

"You need a crowbar," Richard said from behind. Jill hadn't heard him come up, but she wasn't surprised. "And I don't have one," he added.

"I do," called Lisa from the aisle over.

Moments later, Jill slotted the crowbar into the small gap at the left of the door and pushed. The door folded in like an accordion.

"You sure?" asked Richard when no one else spoke. Jill nodded and handed the crowbar to Bri, who stood nearby with unfocused eyes and a pale countenance. Jill entered.

Better Man

LISTEN: To strive. To push, To reach beyond. To manifest the higher. To become the future in the present. To birth a dancing star. These are transcendent values that we strive to embody. Anything less represents failure and betrayal. Death is preferable- for at least in death, one can feed worms.

(a collect from the Liturgy of the Better Man)

A Visit With Friends

"Can I come in?" The curly haired man in the red polo shirt stood at the door. Over his shoulder, Charles could see the golden-red sun setting.

"No," said Charles. "Even if I let you, you know you couldn't stay."

The man in the red shirt looked back. Charles assumed he was looking down the hill, towards the forest behind the cabins. "But," he said, turning again to face forward. "I have no place to go and the sun is setting."

Charles' stomach clenched as he fought back an angry reply. "That's your own fault," he said. "I can't help you."

"But," the red shirt objected.

"No," Charles replied. "No buts. You can't come in and you can't stay here. Good bye." And he shut the door in the face of the red shirted man.

Expedition

It was night. Lightning flashed, thunder cracked, and something burned. Jill shuddered in the corner of a ruined shed. The remaining sliver of roof blocked some of the torrential rain, but did nothing for the freezing wind. Jill blinked and saw that Richard squatted nearby with his rifle gripped in both hands.

"Wha, wha, wha," she stuttered.

"It came apart when you went in," Richard answered. "The second you stepped from the top of the stairs to the inside of that bus."

Jill shivered violently. Water soaked her hair, coat, and everything underneath.

"We need better shelter," said Richard. "Or we'll die." He stood, held the rifle in his right and extended his left to Jill.

Jill hesitated. "Where," she said and spit out a mouthful of water. "Where."

"Are the rest?" Richard said, finishing for her.

"Probably dead. I saw the dogs take Lisa down. The rich girl ran off. I didn't see her boyfriend. The hippie ran for the road. He might of made it." Richard grabbed Jill's elbow. "We have to move or we will die."

Jill allowed Richard to pull her up. Standing hurt. Pain radiated from her hips and knees, and from her feet most of all. She continued shivering. "Hypothermia," Richard said. He still held her arm. "Come on," he said, pulling. Jill followed.

Thick, viscous mud sucked at her boots, threatening to pull them from her feet with every step. Water sloshed up to her ankles and soaked down into her socks. Wind driven rain blinded her and whipped her hair into knotted rats' tails. Richard kept pulling.

Fighting to stay upright, they stumbled and slid down the slope of a barely visible hill. Lightning illuminated great heaps between the bowing trees. Richard turned and pulled her close to one. The water was mid-calf. Up close Jill could see the heap was not a pile of debris or a giant boulder, but rather an artificial thing. Its top was rounded, with a pipe projecting outward. Interlocking gears ran along the side and flat plates threaded along a narrow space along them. Treads. That's what they were.

"Tank," sputtered Jill. She pulled Richard's arm, but he shook his head.

"Duster," he announced over the din of the rain and thunder. "Not tank." He peered around the corner and pushed her down and back, into the treads. "Shhh," he said, holding his finger to his lips.

A rough bark cut through the noise, silencing all for a brief moment. Jill looked to her left, and saw a large dog. It looked like a giant bulldog, with the usual flat nose and muzzle, and unusually large, long, bright white teeth. But the teeth were wrong- twisted and pushed into and around each other, and some shone like... Metal. The dog had jagged strips of metal embedded in its gums. It was growling. Richard pulled her upright.

The growling intensified. It reminded Jill of the sound produced by an idling eighteen-wheeler, or maybe even a tank. The sound came from all directions at once, and as she watched more dogs became visible in the downpour. All showed the same terrible grimace, and on some glistening chunks protruded from heads, backs, and sides. Not one approached, or moved at all, after Jill saw it for the first time.

Richard pulled her around the front of the vehicle. Jill

glanced up to glimpse two parallel pipes on the not-tank's rotunda. And then they were back out, into the mud and now knee-deep water. Jill's body felt clumsy and distant, as though she operated it by remote control. Richard, by contrast, appeared to have total mastery and moved them along at a slow but steady pace, weaving back and forth through rows of what might have been more fighting vehicles, while at the same time avoiding packs of the growling, metal infested, and yet eerily still, dogs.

And then the ground dipped and flattened, and there were no more trees or mounds. The water was mid-thigh. Jill leaned on Richard; she was having trouble staying up, but could not understand why. Lightning flashed, illuminating a wide-open field. In better weather it was probably a pleasant glade, but at present it was a shallow muddy lake. A gray square building occupied the very center. It was sunk unevenly into the water and muck, so that the corner farthest from them was its highest point. The structure itself appeared to be sound. A pitch-black opening on the side facing them was large enough to admit a tall truck. "Garage," Jill thought. "Dry." She attempted to move her legs, and slowly, after a significant delay, they began to respond. Richard cast his left arm across her.

"Dogs," he rasped. And Jill, now refocusing, saw that there were hundreds of the beasts in the field, between them and shelter. They stood still, on the water's surface.

Jill sputtered until Richard shushed her with a hand wave.

WHY said a loud voice from the center of a pack to the right. HAVE YOU COME.

The largest dog yet, this one with metal festooning its body and pushing forth from its eye sockets, stepped forward. Jill shrieked and pulled back. Richard held her.

"We're leaving," answered Richard. "We want to leave."

The massive dog ignored him. YOU ARE KNOWN it said, and they all knew it addressed Jill. Its mouth did not move, but Jill heard the voice, deep and loud.

"St, st," she stuttered in reply.

THE BUS said the voice. THE PROPHET. The beast stepped back a few inches. There was silence. The rain was stopping, but the wind continued to blow. Jill felt her body try to shiver and only achieve a light quiver. She wanted to worry, but felt too sleepy.

"Hey," Richard shook her. "Stand up." Jill fought to

raise her chin. She swayed back and forth in the water. Her legs felt like melting rubber.

GO the beast declared. The dogs began to retreat to the square building. Richard pulled her to the side, up a gradual slope. Thunder echoed. Jill tripped. And then they were gone.

"Hey." She hit something hard and firm, and began to slide. "Hey, hey!" Something clattered and creaked and yellow shone around her. A hand pulled her sideways across slippery wetness and onto something... not wet. Warmer.

"Help me, here," the voice said. Another, smaller dry hand gripped her other arm and they pulled once, then stopped. The clattering and the creak sounded.

"Towels," said the voice. "Just pile them on. I'm not stripping her."

And then they were gone again.

A Visit With Friends

They sat side by side on folding chairs in the basement, keeping watch over the woman under the pile of towels. Richard, having showered, changed clothes, and wrapped a thick blanket around himself, drank scalding hot black coffee from a red ceramic mug.

Next to him, Charles wore his pajama scrubs and waited for the right time to speak.

"You were gone a long time," he said.

Richard remained silent.

"I wasn't sure if you were coming back."

Richard sighed and still said nothing.

"I was scared."

"You should be," Richard replied. He sat motionless for a moment before continuing. "Who visited?"

"Another white coat," answered Charles.

"And?" prompted Richard.

"A founder," said Charles. "Wearing a red shirt." Charles rubbed his chin. "Everybody wants to apologize. They always say, 'I'm sorry.' Sometimes they want me to forgive. I knew he was a founder because he didn't. All he really wanted was to escape."

Expedition

Jill snaked a hand out of her blanket and pulled at her matted hair. "I'm going to have to shave my head," she joked. Charles chuckled. Richard tried to smile. She lounged on a comfortably padded couch, with a cup of steaming coffee next to her elbow on a nearby end table. Charles, thin and pale, sat in an armchair across from her, while Richard paced in front of the room's main entrance.

"We were worried you wouldn't wake up," said Charles.

Jill shrugged.

"I'm going to try and get you out of here, when the sun comes up," said Richard.

"Okay," said Jill. "What time is it?"

Richard shook his head.

"Everything is wrong," explained Charles. "Time goes too fast or too slow. People and places come and go."

"All we can do is wait," interrupted Richard. "There's no way to tell when it will be safe."

"Or if," added Charles.

Jill thought for a moment. "I don't understand," she said, finally.

"We don't either," said Richard.

Charles looked at Richard, who nodded.

"But we can tell you a little," said Charles. "It might be wrong."

Richard came over to the end of the couch and sat down. Jill noted the bags under his eyes and his slouching shoulders.

"We'll tell this like a story," he said to Charles. "Like at bedtime. It could be true, or it could be false." He sighed. "And then we'll all try to get some sleep."

Charles nodded. "You start," Richard said to Charles.

Charles' Story

Once upon a time, a father and son traveled to a distant land, where the father had been called to serve as custodian in the castle of a great king. The father and son were grieving the deaths of the mother and sister, and the father hoped this important job would help them rediscover happiness.

But when they arrived, the castle was mostly empty. The king and all of his court were absent, as were the majority of the subjects. Those remaining could not say where the missing had gone. The castle was in poor repair, and the father immediately took on the responsibility of providing for all as best he could while trying to repair the damage. The son was left by himself to explore.

One day, the son went down into the rooms underneath. Some people call these rooms dungeons, but the son did not because they weren't scary. The rooms were dark, dusty, and damp, and the son did see some rats, but that was all. The floors were even. The ceilings were solid and secure. There were no prison bars, great locking doors, or torture implements. The son was disappointed. But then, at the very end of his visit, when he was preparing to go back up, he found a small door on the side of some stairs. The door was swollen shut, but with a lot of pulling and a little cursing, he managed to open it.

The son found a man inside. It turned out that this man was a personal servant to the missing king. The servant had been starving and came out when the son promised him food. The son fed the servant and then brought him to the father, but the servant would not talk because he was afraid. The father promised not to beat the servant or mistreat him in any way, but the servant would not talk.

Every day, the son would bring the servant to the father, and the servant would refuse to talk, until one day, after many weeks had passed. The father had been working hard at repairing the castle walls to make the people safe. The servant watched the work from the keep but did not help. The day the work was finished, the servant asked the father, "Do you know who broke the

walls?" The father said no. The servant said, "We did."
The father asked why. The servant said, "Some of the
people thought they should be king. Others thought that
there should be no king. But they all agreed that this king
needed to die, so they attacked when they thought he was
sleeping. He wasn't. The king knew their plans, and when
they broke into his room they found it empty, except for a
message written on a slip of paper lying on the royal bed.

"The message said, 'You can have what you want.'

"The attackers fought each other, and the fight spread
through the entire castle. The battle lasted for a day and a
night. When the fighting stopped, bodies lay everywhere
and carnage covered everything. The survivors- the old,
the young, the women, the sick, and the wounded- came
together and made plans to leave. There was too much
death and too much damage for anyone to stay. But
before they could leave, the demons came.

"And that's when I ran to the room where your son
found me. I ate the food I had and hoped I would die."

"What side did you fight on?" the father asked the
servant when he finished his tale.

The servant began to cry. He told the father he'd lied,
that he'd hidden when the fighting started. He begged the

father to spare his life.

"I can't give or take life," said the father. "I'm just a custodian. I can't judge. But answer one more question," he said. "How did you know about the demons?"

"I heard them come," said the servant. "And I felt their footsteps, and I knew their presence. The foulness of a demon is unmistakable."

The father thanked the servant for his honesty and they became friends. From that day forward they worked to repair the castle, together.

Charles nodded to Richard, who continued the story.

Richard's Story

The servant told the truth. The demons were real, and they returned and stole the son. The father left everything and followed them into their own territory. The father couldn't fight them. The demons saw that the father was a brave yet broken man, and took pity on him and gave him his son back. The son's soul had been badly wounded. The son needed light to heal, and because the castle now lay in deep darkness, the father could not take the son back there. They had to go someplace new. Someplace safe.

When he was with the demons the son heard of a place of light and safety on the side of a lake. It was a modest journey, not too far, and so the father took the son to the shore of the lake and they made a home there.

Richard nodded to Jill. "What, me?" she asked.

"Yes, you." said Charles. "It's your turn."

Jill's Story

"Um..." Jill began.

There was a girl. She wasn't a princess or anyone special. She was an ordinary girl with a mom and a dad who lived in an ordinary house in an ordinary neighborhood. One day the mother asked the girl to go look for her uncle. He had gone away and no one knew where. The girl didn't know anything about him. She didn't even know she had an uncle before her mother asked her to do the job.

The girl accepted the job and started looking. She discovered that her uncle had been missing for a long time and that she was not the first person to look. She learned that everyone else had failed. She thought that she was going to fail, too, and then someone said they'd seen him. When the girl asked, it turned out they'd only seen a place where her uncle had been. They hadn't actually seen him. The mother heard the news and told the girl to go, just in case her uncle was there. The girl didn't want to, but she obeyed.

And so it was the girl went to a... dark forest to look for her uncle. She saw the place where her uncle had been, but the place was cursed by magic so she couldn't remember what she saw. The magic was so powerful that she couldn't remember anything for a while, not even her name. Some kind people rescued her and helped her remember who she was.

Jill looked up. "That's my story."

Expedition

Sunlight beamed through the windows on either side of the room. Jill blinked and sat up. Richard, sitting up at the end of the couch, slept with his chin on his chest. Jill noticed that Charles was gone.

Jill discarded her blankets and went exploring. There was a hallway leading out from the room she'd slept in, and two exterior doors along the wall that opened on to a wide porch. Following the hall, Jill found a small kitchen, a long narrow room filled with a table and chairs, a storage closet, a bathroom, stairs leading down, and a small sitting area at the very front. She saw that the building was constructed on the side of a hill and that the first floor was even with the ground in the front and raised over a basement in the back.

"Bedrooms and more storage space down below," croaked Richard. He smiled warmly while leaning on the doorway.

Jill returned the smile. "What's the plan?" she asked.

"To get you out of here," said Richard.

They ate and prepared to leave. Jill wore mismatched clothes recovered from a downstairs closet. "Left by campers," explained Richard. Richard brought his rifle and a pack.

They set out from the front door on the upper level. The sun was bright and the sky was blue. "Don't worry about Charles," Richard said as they stepped out. "I can't explain where he's gone, but I can say he's safe. I'll catch up with him later."

Richard led Jill up the side of the hill and around an elevated white wooden paneled building. "Cafeteria," said Richard. Past that was the parking lot where the group had parked the previous day. Jill was dismayed to see it empty and its gravel unmarked.

"That settles that," remarked Richard. "Maybe the

hippie moved it."

"With no tire marks?" questioned Jill.

"Remember the rain," answered Richard. "On to the chapel."

They turned away from the parking strip and began walking up the hill. "Tell me about your uncle," said Richard.

"What?" asked Jill. "Why?"

"I have something," he said. "It might be his."

Jill sighed. "I don't know much. His name was Jewel, but everyone knew him as Benjy. My grandmother was well educated and loved literature. My grandfather was a banker and loved money. My grandfather was abusive and my grandmother had affairs. She named my uncle after a Faulkner character to get back at him. The rumor was that Jewel was the son of the parish priest. He had developmental problems so she nicknamed him Benjy, who was also a Faulkner character."

"My uncle was bad with people and good with numbers. He was going into banking, and his only friends were the Alphas. He handled their books and they let him hang out, years after graduation. It was no surprise he was on the bus when it disappeared."

Jill finished as they approached the final building. It turned out to be two buildings joined together by covered walkways. One building Richard called the Activity Center. It was a raised, single story structure dominated by one central open room. Smaller storage rooms opened from it, as did a small suite of administrative offices. The second building was an A-frame chapel. The chapel's sharply pitched roof came down to within a foot of the ground. Richard led Jill around to the front, and paused on top of a rectangular concrete slab the length and width of a twin mattress.

"In memory of Teller, Killian, and Bissell," Richard read from the slab. "Dead heroes. The superman is the meaning of the earth. Let your will say: the superman shall be the meaning of the earth!"

"What is that?" asked Jill.

"Read it yourself," said Richard. "It's what's written. I don't know about the second part, but we think the people named were government big shots in the sixties and seventies. Charles thinks Teller was Edward Teller, the nuclear scientist. If that's the case, then I think its possible Killian was James Killian, President Eisenhower's science advisor.

Bissell is probably Richard Bissell, the head of the CIA during the Bay of Pigs."

"Heroes?" asked Jill.

"What it says," answered Richard. "Charles has theories. You'd have to ask him. Anyway, let's get inside."

The chapel's wooden double doors were unlocked, but swollen shut. Richard dragged one side open and they stepped inside.

Chapel

The air was hot and stale. Sweat coated Jill's body.

"What are we doing here?" she asked, while looking around the barren interior. Signs and symbols drawn in chalk, charcoal, and salt covered the floor, save for a circle on a raised dais where the altar had been.

"This is where I found the things from your uncle," Richard explained. "Charles thinks this is where everything started."

"What started?" Jill asked.

Richard shook his head.

"I don't understand," said Jill.

"Right," said Richard.

They stood in silence, and then she asked, "How are my uncle and the bus connected with this?"

"Simple," said Richard. "The Alphas drove the bus here, and your uncle was on it." He grinned and continued, "There's no good explanation. Nothing makes sense."

"So the tanks? The dogs?"

"Yeah," he grunted. "But those were Dusters, not tanks. They're tracked machines with big machine guns. They were used in Korea and Vietnam."

"Helpful," she quipped.

Richard brought a manila folder out of his pack. "This is your uncle's," he explained. "I'll hold on to it for now."

Jill nodded. "All right. What's next?"

"It's more than two hours to hike to the border," said Richard. "It would be best to find a car. I was hoping we'd find your ride on the hill. I'm still hoping the hippie moved it."

"Why?" she asked.

"We're leaving," said Richard.

Journal

[text from the first page]
Daytime.

Everyone is gone. The president and his woman went into the forest a few days ago. I don't know what they want to find. The others went in ones, twos, and even threes. Most went north, across the road. The rest went east, along the road. Only the president and his consort went south, away from the road. I think they lost hope.

As for me, there's canned food in the infirmary. Every few days it's replenished. I sleep and eat know not Ulysses. Sometimes I stay in the chapel. Other times I walk behind the cabins along the edge of the forest. I've been thinking of walking around the lake. I think it would be safe.

Expedition

There was a dog in the road. Jill had convinced herself the earlier encounter was imaginary, but here one was in broad daylight. It straddled the cracked and faded yellow center line, but this time, remained silent. Mid-morning sun reflected from countless shards of metal protruding from its back and sides, but especially from its eye sockets.

Jill and Richard froze.

"Where'd that come from?" Jill asked. "It just..."

"Crap," Richard answered.

Jill followed Richard's gaze. There was another one behind them. Its eyes were intact, and instead a large mass of twisted metal bulged from both sides of its muzzle. They were cut off.

"Oh," she said.

"Don't worry," called a voice.

Thick forest came within five feet of either side of the road, and bright sunlight hid everything behind the tree line in deep shadow. Richard and Jill were unwilling to look away from the beasts. Richard pulled his rifle up to his shoulder and put his finger on the trigger.

"Don't worry," the voice repeated. "They won't hurt you."

A child stepped out of the forest to Jill's left, behind the eyeless beast. The child was short, with black hair and brown skin. He wore shorts and a t-shirt, and his feet were bare. Jill guessed he was ten years old.

"I'm Jose," he said, and he placed his hand on the eyeless beast's head. "What's your name?"

Jill hesitated.

"That's Jill," Richard said to Jose. "We've met before," he explained to Jill.

"Yes," confirmed Jose. "I need you," he said to Jill.

"What?"

"I need you," Jose repeated.

"For what?" she asked. "To do what?"

"Follow the dogs," said Jose. "They won't hurt you if you obey. And lower the gun, Richard."

Richard complied.

Journal

[The second page is quartered into four equal parts, and each quarter contains a figure, clearly labeled in bold text. The top left drawing depicts a man sitting on the ground, scraping himself with rocks. The name under the figure reads JOB. The top right drawing shows a man chained to a rock. A bird perches on the man's chest, and pecks at his abdomen. The name under this figure reads PROMETHEUS. The bottom left drawing shows a man pushing a rock up an incline. The name under this drawing reads SISYPHUS. The final drawing on the bottom right shows a man holding a human arm and head.

The name under this drawing reads FRANKENSTEIN.]
[Text on the third page]

The God came from the forest to talk. "Write," He said, and I wrote.

"You will be my prophet, but not as those who came before. Those wrote of what they saw to warn Israel because there was hope. Israel is gone. The people believe they have changed, but their hearts remain. Their sins cry out to Heaven. The Heaven they have rejected. Yet hope endures.

"You will travel the land and tell. You will speak to those who come. And you will write."

[Text on the fourth page]

ST. JOB

Served. God wagered. Job endured.

ST. PROMETHEUS

Bridged. God tortured. Prometheus endured.

ST. SISYPHUS

Challenged. God crushed. Sisyphus endured.

ST. FRANKENSTEIN

Surpassed. God ignored. Frankenstein endured.

And now ST. JEWEL, or BENJY the LESS. I stand

in the ashes and bear witness. I speak with the innocent, both young and old. The innocent you tortured.

Expedition

The eyeless beast walked in front. Jill followed with Richard after and the beast with the monstrous mouth coming last of all. Richard carried his rifle in both hands, with the muzzle pointing down and to the left.

They walked at a steady, yet manageable pace, down one hill and then up another. They wound around trees and patches of thick foliage, taking periodic breaks to allow the humans to catch their breaths.

The beasts remained mute and made so little noise while walking that Jill wondered if they were real. "Is this all in my head?" she asked.

"I'm here," replied Richard, close behind.

"But what about them?" she asked.

"Ours is not to reason or to question why," answered Richard.

"Not helpful," she said, and lapsed into silence.

They stopped in at the trunk of a large felled tree, and the beasts lay down on their stomachs.

"What now?" asked Jill. No answer came. Richard

gently set his rifle down and then sat on the soft, leaf strewn ground. After a minute, Jill joined him.

"We came into this in the south," said Richard. "I worked maintenance at this gated community."

"Demons?" asked Jill.

Richard shook his head. "Yes and no. Something was wrong and Charles went missing. That kid," Richard pointed out into the forest, "Jose was there."

"Then what?" Jill asked when Richard failed to continue.

"I found him and we came here. I don't know how long it's been."

"How does this end?" Jill whispered.

Richard shook his head again. "Don't know." He sighed. "Will it?"

The beasts stood, and they did likewise. The eyeless beast resumed walking, and they followed.

Journal

[text on the fifth page]

> Lamentation of ST. BENJY the LESS.
> In the manor,
> Anxiety stalks ruined walls and empty buildings.
> Under the bitter plains,

Children speak the language of birds.

In the arcade,

Abandoned traps capture youth.

In the forest,

Men walk in the form of dogs,

The pools are empty but yet still full.

Why strive?

Why endure?

Are you happy?

Expedition

Jill sobbed. Richard grimaced.

They stood at one end of an oval clearing. Two bodies lay side by side on their backs before them. A burlap bag lay to one side. A white pickup truck was parked at the far end of the clearing, in front of an overgrown yet passable rutted dirt road that led out, through the forest.

The beast with the grotesque mouth stood between them and the truck. The eyeless beast drew near to Jill.

Jill ignored it, and continued crying for the dead. One was Lisa, the tour guide. Her right arm was missing at the elbow, and her body was stained red-brown from the waist down. The other was Aiden, the boyfriend. His throat had been torn out, and his chest and stomach were rust red. Their arms (or their stumps, in Lisa's case) were laid along their bodies, and their legs were placed together with their feet up. Their eyes and mouths were closed, and had their bodies not borne such obvious injuries, Jill would have thought they were sleeping.

Richard opened the bag and peeked inside. "Rags," he said, and then, after reaching in, recoiled and added, "Bones. There's a skull."

PROPHET said the eyeless beast. BURY.

"My uncle?" Jill squeaked.

BURY the beast repeated. The second beast moved to allow passage to the truck, and Richard walked over and looked in the bed. "Shovel," he announced, and he brought it over.

Jill cried while Richard dug near the center of the clearing. "The bodies too, or just the bag?" he asked after his second shovelful.

PROPHET the beast answered.

Richard shrugged and continued digging.

Jill wiped her tears and began taking turns. Sweat soaked their clothes, the pile of dirt grew, and the hole deepened, yet the sun never appeared to move. When the hole was deep enough, they buried the bag under a thick layer of dirt. Filling the hole went faster than the dig, but even so Jill felt so much time had passed the day should be ending.

"Sun's the same," Richard commented.

STONES said the beast.

"What?" asked Richard.

"Stones," said a voice from the forest. "For a marker. To let people know." Jose stepped into the clearing and the beasts left.

Richard dropped the shovel, and pointed with his right hand. Jill thought he was going to argue. She reached out, touched his elbow, and he lowered the hand. "Just do it," she whispered. Together, they picked out natural stones, chunks of concrete, and bits of broken brick from the tall grass, and piled them where they buried the bag. They stopped when the pile was waist high to Jill. And still, the sun had not moved. Jill felt faint and unsteady, and she leaned on Richard.

Jose stood where he'd been since he first emerged. Exhausted, both physically and emotionally, Jill mustered a final effort. "Why do you care?" she asked with a slight tinge of passion.

"We're sorry," answered Jose. "He was nice."

"What are you?" she countered, raising her voice.

Jose remained silent. Jill pushed off from Richard to stand upright, and stared at the child, confusion and pain radiating outward.

"I," Jose began, "Speak for the children. I..." his voice trembled, "am the children. I am, and we are, what's left."

Jill began to wobble and Richard caught her.

"You need to leave," said Jose, in a stronger voice. "Take the truck. The dirt road will come out near the parking lot. The sun will hold for as long as you need. We're sorry. And we thank you."

Jose returned to the forest as Richard guided Jill to the truck.

Journal

[The sixth and final page is a map of Brown Lake.]

The kidney shaped lake occupies the center of the page. The camp (chapel, activity center, cafeteria, infirmary and cabins) is on its north shore. Forest surrounds the lake on the west, east, and south. DOGS ARE HERE is written in the bottom right corner. There is a small cross above the words DOGS and the words "my place" scrawled next to it in barely legible script. CAR GRAVEYARD/ PARKING LOT is written in the open space above the word DOGS. A road snakes from side to side along the top edge of the map.

At the Border

Richard parked the truck in a wide gravel lot, just over the border. Jill slumped against the passenger side door, deep asleep. Drool leaked from the corner of her mouth and pooled in a dark, damp circle on the shoulder of her shirt. She did not stir when Richard slammed the door behind him and walked towards the two figures waiting in the shade at the lot's edge.

One of the figures was a smartly dressed gray haired woman in a business suit. The other was a uniformed police officer.

"I'm Dr. Core," said the gray-haired woman. "Are they in the truck bed?"

Richard nodded.

"The officer will take care of things if you'll leave the truck here."

"What about Jill?" he asked.

"She comes with me. Or us, if you want."

Richard grimaced. "Charlie," he said.

"You don't know he'll be there."

"You don't know he won't."

Dr. Core pointed across the road to a brown Volvo. "Then take my car. The keys are in it."

Richard did not look back, but walked directly to the car. Gravel crunched as the police officer brought Jill to a stop nearby.

"Richard," Jill whispered as she watched him drive away.

"He's devoted," commented Dr. Core. Dr. Core gestured towards the shade, and together she and the officer walked Jill out of the sun.

"Sunburn, dehydration, and old-fashioned exhaustion," said the doctor. "But no significant injuries. We'll run a psych evaluation later."

"What?" slurred Jill, in a weak voice.

"It's finished," said the doctor. "It's time to go home."

Visit with Friends

The curly haired man in the red shirt was still there in the morning, huddled in the corner of the porch, looking at nothing and no one. Charles brought a book of poetry and read aloud as the sun rose.

> "Little lamb, who made thee?
> Dost thou know who made thee?
> Gave thee life and bid thee feed.
> By the stream and o'er the mead;
> Gave thee clothing of delight,
> Softest clothing wooly bright;
> Gave thee such a tender voice,
> Making all the vales rejoice!
> Little lamb, who made thee?
> Dost thou know who made thee?"

The man looked up. "God therefore cannot hurt ye, and be just," he replied. "Not just, not God; not feared then, nor obeyed: Your fear itself of death removes the fear. Why then was this forbid? Why but to awe, why but to keep ye low and ignorant, His worshippers."

They stared at each other in silence. Charles closed the book and went inside.

About the author:

Michael Bertrand lives in Wisconsin
with his wife and four children.

He enjoys mangling philosophy and
confusing people when he isn't working
the night shift at a 30-day AODA rehab.

This is his first novel.